PLACES OF POWER

BY LONDON STUDENTS

A GOLD SCHOOLS ANTHOLOGY

Copyright © Gold Schools Publishing, London UK, f.gilbert@gold.ac.uk British Library Cataloguing-in-Publications Data A catalogue record for this book is available from the British Library.

Dedication
For all London students who want to be, or already are, creative writers.

Acknowledgments

Thanks to Sam Sullivan at Newington Design, the book and cover designer; the magnificent Widening Participation Team at Goldsmiths, Laura Nicholson, Sam Kelly and Goldsmiths, University of London for funding this project; thanks to all the committed teachers at Beal High School, Conisborough College, Deptford Green, Eltham Hill, Forest Hill School, Hampstead School, Harlington,, Stepney Green, Walworth Academy for enabling the project to happen; huge thanks to all the Goldsmiths post-graduate students who worked so hard to make the anthology a reality; and, last but not least, thanks to all the secondary school students who took part.

ISBN-13: 978-1725004948
ISBN-10: 1725004941

CONTENTS

INTRODUCTION

Welcome to the third Gold Schools Anthology!

This marvellous new anthology is a collection of pieces written by secondary & primary school students from a varied range of London state schools. Having been given the theme of 'Places of Power by Goldsmiths' Department of Educational Studies, these pupils wrote movingly about their lives, dreams and ambitions in the form of poems, fictional extracts and autobiographical accounts. They were assisted by their teachers as well as creative writing post-graduate students & PGCE English students at Goldsmiths.

The book is not only required reading for anyone who wants to learn about young people's lives, but it's also a wonderful resource for teachers who wish to inspire their pupils to write in a similar vein.

You can watch the video that kicked off the first anthology here:

https://youtu.be/WU7z4Qv_FiA

And find out more about the various activities going on the MA in Creative Writing and Education & PGCE English programme which hosts the anthology at these links:

Official Goldsmiths' websites:

http://www.gold.ac.uk/pgce/secondary-english/
http://www.gold.ac.uk/pg/ma-creative-writing-education/

Unofficial blogs:

https://creativewritingandeducation.wordpress.com/
https://a2zofenglishteaching.wordpress.com/

The anthology is published through Print on Demand which means if there are any mistakes or omissions, they can be quickly rectified. Please email me if you spot anything: **sir@francisgilbert.co.uk**

Francis Gilbert, July 2018

BEAL HIGH SCHOOL

Cages

by Safiyah Ali

This is the eternity world. We live in a world of separation. Living amongst the poor or the very rich. Or me, an outcast, made to be both and looked down upon. Made to live in the cages. My world of separation is large and the idea of money divides us as though we're like different species. And here I am hidden away in the shadows.

They name you demon and treat you like one too. You know nothing about your parents! Living in a world like this something has to change. So today I stand chained, tied to this cage with an over powering feeling of anger. That has built up in me for so long. I'm going to show the world that I'm not a nobody. I can already feel the taste of freedom on the tip of my tongue and the feeling of power in my legs ready to sprint. I'm ready to break away from the cage and I will do it today because I am the power in my powerful place.

Nibiru

By Simeon Tsenov

There is a planet somewhere in our galaxy called Nibiru which is identical to our planet. The same food, countries, people, animals...but there is one immeasurable difference! This planet has no money, but it is still happy. Has no king or queen but still makes life changing decisions. Has no rules but is still filled with people on their best behaviour. Most importantly, it has no evil. This means no murder, no terrorism, and no tragedies.

Fortunately us humans haven't discovered this planet and hopefully never will. Planet Nibiru lives in total peace everyone is treated equally. If we humans ever discover planet Nibiru and land there, we will ruin the everlasting peace. Us humans are very greedy and if we steal from them, the Nibirus might fight back and spark and war between the two worlds. Humans may capture some Nibirus and turn them into slaves on our planet.

But the Nibirus will have something that humans will never have- humanity, forgiveness and kindness.

The Galaxy

By Ragu Datt

The galaxy is an endless mystery. Who made it and why? Did they make it for our benefit, or did they plan a devious game where we worship them but then they're secretly a villain and press a bright yellow button and blow up earth?

Wait. Why only earth? There are people on other planets as well. Aren't there? What we call extra-terrestrial life forms. What about them? What if they're the genius' living on Saturn observing us, thinking we're the odd creatures? Saturn. Why does Saturn have a ring?

Why doesn't Mars have a ring? Mars...mmm! Why did they name the chocolate bar after the planet? Not just Mars. There's Galaxy and Milky Way. What's the deal with space and chocolate? Even the stars look like pieces of minute chocolate chips. I bet on Jupiter you get a great view of these. Jupiter.

It's so immense! Colossal! It's massive compared to Pluto. Pluto is such a dwarfed planet. Well, now I feel like a hypocrite. I've always thought that you shouldn't judge something by its size. I totally disagreed when I found that astronomers declared Pluto was not a planet anymore, just because it was too microscopic.

What if an adult was too small? Would they not be allowed to be an adult because of their height? If all adults were tall, then astrologists would have already seen past the Moon with just a naked eye. The moon....

I'd love to hover over the moon. In the news you always hear 'man on the moon' but have you ever heard 'Woman on the moon?' Isn't that sexist? Well, all I know is that I want to be the future's first ever 'Child on the moon!' I will hike up the powerful Mercury, study a star, race a bumpy meteor, but I will make it (eventually).

Well I'll be off now. I shall drift into my astronomical thoughts....

The Sequel: Power

By Tyresa Pakeerathan.

Power – what a valid word! Power cannot be categorised as good or bad and comes in many forms. From a bulky brown trunk to a strong secure bridge.

> Power is a beautiful thing when it wants to be,
> But easily loses its charm when it is abused,

Power in wrong hands can make the innocent bruised,
But free the innocent before they lie under the yew tree.

The past cannot be changed,
The future is yet in your power,
It is you, who decides to make it sweet or sour,
Let not the future be deranged.

With that said,
Let's talk about the places of power!
Is yours an elegant ivory tower?
Or a cosy comfortable camp bed?

Well mine is a kin to a temple,
Where I found answers to my prayers,
It is made from several bricklayers,
Mala Yusoufzai used this weapon yet so simple.

Nelson Mandela took this weapon as his battle,
Martin Luther King helped provide the African American's with this,
It gave us children bliss,
Nothing can keep us safe on this ride than this saddle.

My house of God equips you with this,
It is your essential kit,
It lets you gain your wit,
Do not let this mess.

When my beloved father died,
He would always say,
That education was my leeway,
And even though he is gone I should hold onto his pride.

Others believe that I am a failure,
Some bite their tongue,
But remember: heroes are always unsung,
My mother would tell me let success be their saviour.

So, what is my place of power?
As you might have guessed,
The secret is undressed,
My school is my tower.

BLACKFEN SCHOOL

HAIKUS

Sunset.

By Santiya Manivannan.

Walking down the isle
Watching this sunset go down
Everything so quiet.

Fireworks.

By Santiya Manivannan.

Red, orange, pink, blue
Give happiness to us all
Faces all lit up.

POETRY

Walking.

By Santiya Manivannan.

Woosh! Woosh!
The trees dance
Never alone, never together
As mice tiptoe, crunching the leaves

The trees snatch the sunlight
Hoot! Hoot! An owl howls, giving me a suspicious eye
I walk carefully through the forest
People rarely wander, but I love to explore

Not far off sits a small cottage where I can rest
Woosh! Woosh
The trees dance
Never alone, never together,
Telling me to turn back, and not to enter.

The Beach.

By Santiya Manivannan.

Hand in hand we delicately walk
Letting our feet melt into the sand
Not even a sound is heard
But for the gentle dance of the waves.

Graveyard.

By Santiya Manivannan.

The dead lonely trees surround me
Branches that move from all directions.
The sky seems so threatening
Yet gloomy at the same time.

"Wait, where am I?"

Dismal, silence, isolation.
The dead leaves on the ground rustle in the silence.
The breeze seems so cold, as if from somewhere unknown.
As the wind starts to howl, sending shivers down my spine.

"Wait, where am I?"

The spirits hang around
Making no sound
Wondering why I'm here
"Come to us"
They say it so clear

Dead bodies lie in their graves
These are the bodies of the dead.
Where have I gone, on my innocent walk?

Snow day.

By Santiya Manivannan.

Looking down, beneath my feet,
There lies the white, colourless snow.
My heart beats calmly and slow
As my tongue emerges from my lips
A small snowflake lands peacefully
And dissolves from the warmth of my body.

SHORT STORIES

The Lighthouse.

By Santiya Manivannan.

I want to tell you what happened. But I haven't got long left. I still don't fully understand what happened. Maybe I never will.

Why did I even go in to the lighthouse? It was one of those days when it's best to stay at home, because everything was going to turn out badly.

"Mum where are we going in this weather?"

"We're going on a car trip"

After a long 4- hour car drive we were finally here. We drove past the lighthouse. It was dilapidated.

We stayed in a cottage near the lighthouse. I desperately wanted to visit it, my curiosity twinging the muscles in my legs to move. So I went out and eventually found my way. As I approached the lighthouse, I could gradually taste more of the saline air with each breath. The furious ocean pounded rocks as if it wished to scatter them. I looked again at the towering dark structure, with its single blinking eye. The lighthouse stood tall on the rocky shore, its paint black and white as if it were a prisoner there- standing isolated in its jailhouse clothes. I stared through the narrow window. I saw the twisting never ending stairs. I placed my left foot... The light started to flicker on and off. I placed my right foot. The light completely turned off. I was in the lighthouse.

Slowly, I climbed up the stairs with caution. A strong wind blew past me. Pitter! Pat! Raindrops fell on my face. I hurriedly brushed the drops off my face. Strangely, the raindrops felt thick, and smelt like copper. There was something within the lighthouse that was dragging me to the top. From nowhere I slipped into a puddle, dropping my torch. As I picked it up and inspected the puddle I became confused. The puddle was red.

What was the red liquid?

I climbed up even further. I finally made it to the small room at the top. I switched on the light.

The room was empty. The paint was peeling, and it looked like nobody had been in here before. As I inspected the room, I saw handprints and numbers. I carefully shined my torch on the wall. It read: "Get me out of here."

Shocked, I ran down the endless stairs. The puddle... it must have been ... BLOOD!

I raced down the stairs to get out of the lighthouse, but the tides were so high, the lighthouse had become its own island. The wind blew harder and it began to thunder. A silhouette appeared. My heart skipped a beat. After every flash of lightening it seemed to move closer. What should I do? The storm was getting rough, as the waves slapped the lighthouse.

I'm trapped.

The Prison Cell.

By Varunegha Sureskumar.

The walls closed in. I couldn't escape the darkness. I sat in the corner of my room, seeing the sharp corners at each edge. The walls, painted red many years ago, connected at each corner, forming a perfect square shaped room. The four walls carried with them so many memories, where many aimless psychotic men had scratched their fingers to the bone. As I looked up, my light flickered as myriad moths fluttered around it, like that was my only hope. The air inside was different. No stimulation. Surrounded by four walls, there was nothing else to do but stare constantly at them. The paint started to chip off as time moved on. On the walls were pipes, which led to rooms where many had been tortured. Ten minutes later, the morning shift had begun. The screams were layered, one on top of each other; a gruesome choir of pain, piercing screams of tortured inmates.

I realised I was breathing through my mouth, because my face and body had been brutally beaten. I couldn't move. Everything looked red, but in a blurry vision, I began to realise... I was one of them.

CONISBOROUGH COLLEGE

Location

By Alexander Kirby, Year 8

Find an empty place – dilapidated and an eyesore – and create something marvellous. It sits there between two terraces of plain and boring houses. Invaded by nature the weeds grow tall and strong, but the grass towers over them, ruling the space. Vibrant shades of green cover the area, creating almost a dense jungle. It is an eyesore, sticking out from all the plain houses like the jumbled mess it is. Without thought people toss their rubbish in there to slowly rot, thinking that someone will collect it; no one ever does. Slowly and surely piles of rubbish stick out like eyesores in the dense green land. It is as ugly as an imaginary monster and it just keeps growing, growing, never stopping or being taken away. The poor plants try to grow large but the dirt and grime stop them from ever reaching their potential.

The area needs to be improved. It could be turned into a beautiful café. People could go there to meet up and just appreciate the beautiful land they have been given. The café would be a fantastic star being born. To create such a fine structure you would first need to cut down the grass and kill the weeds so people will see it looks nice and amazingly neat. Then the piles of horrible rubbish need to be scooped up and taken away so no one has to see those terrible things ever again. Then large handfuls of metal framework need to be added in to support such a heart-warming place. After this add a sprinkle of wooden floor so people don't have to hurt their feet on the uneven and unwanted weeds. Sprinkle down cement and watch shiny stone walls rise higher than the weeds or rubbish ever could. Now a swipe of the hand and the top is covered with a red slate roof and the exterior is complete. Add a pinch of tables and chairs so people can rest up, relax and enjoy themselves in this once dilapidated place. On the outside sprinkle down a couple dozen people to use and enjoy the café. Finally add half a teaspoon of a sign that welcomes all to share in a friendly café for the people.

Timely Reflections

By Sumayyah Sadeer, Year 9

Fluid calm is the horizon of warm, dark tones of reflection
Reflection is the warm, dark tones of horizon
Horizons are endless
So is my mind
My mind? What is my mind?
My mind can be the infinite space of reflection and thought
My mind can be a large space filled with racing thoughts and edging escapes.
Never closed, always flooded
Like a waterfall gushing its water my mind gushes out its words.
Once the thought train leaves, my mind space shuts down
Keep the train moving
No fighting, no shouting, none of it.
The feelings have lifted
The time has gone
Tick, tick, tick- ticking clock or ticking time bomb.
Slowly coming to a peaceful end
A peaceful end of wholesome serenity
And wholesome serenity replaced by chaos
By chaos being picked apart into little fragments of emotion
That emotion floats as if on water through my mind, through my timely reflection.

Happiness

Amber Cray, Year 7

Happiness sounds like a distant angel in the sky waiting to be found,
Other than that I can't hear a sound.
My happy place is not that far away.
Because I go there every day.
My happy place feels very calm,
And you can see a charm.
My happy place smells quite sweet,
And all you do is take a seat.
My happy place is nice,
You don't think about it twice.
My happy place is my parents' room,
And you'll be there in a zoom.
My happy place has a heart,
This is the end, not the start.

Once upon a time

By Siobhan Cardy, Year 9

Once upon a time,
I was happy at home,
Not worrying about a dime.
Where did it all go?

Once upon a time,
I snuggled up in bed,
And didn't care what was ahead.
Where did it all go?

Once upon a time,
I used to be kitchen living
with fruit bowls that had lemons and limes.
Where did it all go?

Once upon a time,
School was a place of fun,
Every lesson would be sublime.
Where did it all go?

Once upon a time,
People would love to laugh
Class was happy and nobody hurt.
Where did it all go?

Once upon a time
Happiness would stay,
School gave us dinner on a plate.
Where did it all go?

Once upon a time,
It all went wrong.

Light on my back

By Joanna Tsitashvili, Year 7

Light on my back, so light that it lightens out the heavy things I've been carrying around. It sings as if there are no worries in the world, no melancholic places, that's what happiness sounds like. As I walk through the fabulous park, my heart is filled with joy and happiness, my fingers start to tingle, my feet start to feel much lighter and I start to smile. As this happens I realise how cruelly pathetic it is that I allowed myself to feel any other emotion that us not jubilance. The smell of candyfloss fills my nostrils. The sight of the beautiful flowers mesmerises my eyes and the sound of the waterfall trickling into the river make a calming state in my mind. It feels like I'm floating, as if all the worries in my life are now below me, the feeling floats me up so high that I can see the whole park in a bird's eye view. This is where I want to stay, now I can't hear what anyone has to say.

Anticipation

By Nesrine Zigadi, Year 8

The anticipation of travelling had been eating me alive ever since I found out my family and I were going to France; asking us that day not to be excited was like trying to ask a fire not to burn. Our eyes were alight, every muscle needed to move, to dance, to jump. I could imagine everything I wanted to see and so right there and then – the sand softly golden with just the right comforting warmth; to rest on the beach feels like a cosy hug, one only matched by the sunshine filled sky, and with tanned legs curled under dusted with sand like flour on bread, I sit close to the lapping waves.

The anticipation was a nervous kind of energy. It tingled through me like electrical sparks on the way to the ground, gathering in my toes. And then it was that first breath that I take as I step out of the airplane full of the Mediterranean cuisine and heat, that had already coated my skin.

As I woke up the morning after a gush of steady wind as long as a heavy sigh poured direct out of the quarter of the morning, with a song that made even the trees dance. We ate croissants on the way, the butter melting as we walked along to the centre of the city: my little brother's fingers were sticky and we laughed as he licked each one clean.

I adored the city, it was effortlessly striking and picturesque, it was a contemporary modern city with an ancient twist. Passing by and gazing at the various monuments that were perfectly painted across the once blank canvas of a city made me feel so elated, and looking out on the street was like looking at the shelf of a busy bookshop, thousands of stores packed together, none of them connected to each other, some big, some small. Walking along the road, I took a deep breath and smelt a sweet, flowery perfume wafting out of a small perfume stand. I picked up a rose and plunged my face deep into its cool damp petals. The rose had caught the heel of my thumb and a streak of blood cried onto my sleeve, yet I had hardly noticed.

The scenery had appealed to me a lot, especially the beach. As the sun scorched our bodies to a crisp, a fiesta of scents was roaming through the entire beach, and I wasn't the only one to notice them. Our stomachs rumbled and growled, hunger crawls at your grumbling belly, it tugs at your intestine which begins to twitch, aching to be fed.

It was loud, it was colourful, and the various grand smells ran through our noses quicker than the water that erupted from the waterfalls. The tall black buildings towered over the people that hid below and the white sky.

The waves were crawling gently to the shore. the ocean was forging its own sea-song. There was a broad streak of orange melting into gold along the waves of the sea. It was a watery wonderland and the beach was drenched in lightening golden haze; the dreamy sea has a rhythmic pulse to it unmatched by any other part of nature.

As I stroll onwards onto the exquisite velvet blanket.

As I take a step toward the spectacular scenery, the blanket subsides beneath my feet.

As I gaze around trying to take in the divine world that encloses me.

My breath steamed against the air and the deafening silence was broken by the sizzling of the griddle.

It's not often you get to see a sunset-gold beach, that was our privilege and as we gazed out to the slothful sea.

DEPTFORD GREEN

The Vikings V South London

A play by Reuben Webster-Reid

Kwengface: Yo brudda

Trizzac: Aye yo have you heard the news from the mandem

Kwengface: Nah fam what they saying doe

Trizzac: Apparently them Viking boys take back the ends

Kwengface: Something let me get the mandem and we can sort them

LR: Aye Karrma, Trizzac and Kwengface are comings to the ends these Vikings are about to regret dis.
Karma: Cool it`s time to ride again

Kwengface: About time we got here bro

Trizzac: Shut up get out the car

All of them: yo bro

Trizzac: I'm done with the chit chat let's get straight to it

Kwengface: Cool so basically Peckham is our ends and the Vikings think this is ice age we not goanna have it

Karma: Word

All four of them wait and camp all night waiting for the Vikings to come and at 7:30 they appear, looking as if they had a hunch back. They are very muscled and beastly, ready for a fight.
Sitting down on the wall Kwengface, Trizzac, Karma and LR came out lurking.

THE VIKINGS: who is't art thee? [who are you?]

Astrid: wherefore art thee? [why are you here?]

Kwengface: Not having dis

Karma: Common look at dem I swear there some Shakespearian guys

Trizzac: I'm ready kweng Peckham is my area this is my ends

Out of nowhere Viking number 2 rapidly struck trizzac with its axe and as the clock struck 9 o'clock the Vikings used the darkness to their advantages.

LR: they got away

Karma: that's not the point at the moment Trizzac is laying on the floor

As Kwengface attended to Trizzac he was aided to LR's house.

Karma: he won't be able to come with us it's now three against one. But the three boys were in for a big surprise because the two Vikings were ready for a war.

The next day on Bird in Bush road the Vikings waiting for Karma to enter the chicken shop. as he entered there was nobody at the till. DING-A LING-A LING! Goes the bell as two hunched massive shadows overwhelmed Karma and as he leisurely turns his head. Three axes where swung into the air.

Suddenly, the window smashes. It is LR coming to save Karma!

Karma: Safe bro, how is there two of them now?

LR: They're growing...
In the corner of Karma's eye there was a note on the floor as he picked it up on there said 'meet us 5 in the park'.
In the park. At night.
Kwengface, LR and Karma are sitting and waiting impatiently for the Vikings. Suddenly the Viking ambush them.
Kwengface attack the first Viking, striking him. The Viking is unaffected. Five patronizing shadows emerged from behind the Viking and he grins. Karma hiding in the tree jumping from behind and was struck with an axe. Trizzac saw from the park at LRs house and with all his strength managed to get down the stairs and managed to get to the park and because of the stroke of the axe that hit his heart it gave him powers and he was able to chop of the head of the Vikings and buried them in the park.
All the scars vanished and Peckham belonged to Zone 2 once more...

Reuben says: I wrote this play to explore the idea that people can always defend their area, just because they live here. They do have a right to protect their area as they have adapted to it after living here for a long time. I made Vikings come back so it was fictional warfare rather than the real gang violence that happens here sometimes so it a 'world gone wrong' because it is gang fighting and also time travel.

Dave's Dystopia

By Dave Liu

In a world without feelings, you wouldn't be able to see the difference between things. Apples and grapes would all look the same. Without any feelings, you'll never feel connected to anything, anything from your childhood, or anything that you like or want to get. You'll never feel the drive to want anything else.

****

I open the door and enter my messy, small house. The walls are white and scribbled on with old games of noughts and crosses. A lonely football rolls forlornly against the door as I squeeze in. I walk into the kitchen and see my 3 younger brothers sitting there still and quiet.

"I am so much better at Fifa than you lot!" I say, trying to make them react, to make them show some sort of feeling. They sit, silent as Nelson's column at 3am on a cold Tuesday morning. I remember how they used to be; loud, destructive. They took things of mine without asking, which made me angry! They spoke loudly, deafeningly, which I couldn't even escape from because I shared a room with them. It made me feel like I was in a never ending pitch black tunnel.

But now, here they sit. Empty shells of their former selves.

I move round them and look out into the yard. My dad stands, still as brickwork. Looking at nothing. In the past, he would never be in at this time. He worked a lot, worked hard, all night until early morning. He was always thinking about something, he was intensely focussed, intelligent.

Now I see him staring blankly at empty air. His hands hanging lifelessly by his side.

World Gone Wrong

By Alain Seri

Once upon a time there was a boy called Jack.
He had a friend called Tom and they were both scary. One day they brought a Ouija board. They went home to test it out. After five minutes they started to hear some creepy footsteps, getting louder and louder. BANG! The lights turn off. Then they heard screaming. They were so scared they called their parents. Then the parents called the police, and the police came.
The friends started to cry and told them everything. But the world was never the same again.

Discrimination

By Jayden Monteiro and Micheal N'Guessan

People in this world discriminate
Why are people filled with such hate?
They care about your ethnicity
But they should practise simplicity
Everyone should have a right
I'll stand up and help you fight
They hate the colour of your skin
Let's stick together and help you win
You still wonder what they think
Even when you're on the brink
Just take time to say 'HI'
We are all under the same sky

Commentary

Michael says: We wrote this poem because we feel like discrimination is a huge, common issue in the world today. It affects many people in many ways that also affect the world itself.
Jayden says: We wrote this so everyone can treat each other's right and to show love and equality.

Gangs

By Kenny Adekunle

Everyday people are dying,
Just because of knives people are crying.
Stabs. Jabs.
Guns are not fun.
Taking someone's life is just wrong.

Think about it like this a loaf of bread;
Getting cut everyday like a stab to the head.
Drugs:
why couldn't you just ask for a hug
or a mug?

Where does all this money come from?
Gangs are formed for money that is illegal,
when you could have done something legal.

Contrast Means Opposite of Something

By John Kirkum

Up and down,
left and right,
white to black,
short and tall,
red and blue,
 they all contrast without a clue

from dusk to dawn
to brains to brawn
to ping to pong
ding dong
while I sing a song

Commentary

John Says: In my poem it's worlds gone wrong because in the light is a display of good but dark is a presentation of bad and both behaviour and colours both contrast and that is what the world is like right now.

Most expensive year on record for US natural disasters

Jacob Williams reports:

Hurricane Harvey caused damage estimated at around $125bn in Texas last year

Total losses amounted to $306bn the agency said, over $90bn more than the previous record set in 2005.

Last year there were 16 separate disasters that costed over $1bn.

However, scientists were quick to point out that cold spells do occur even if the overall temperature trend is rising, leaving America questioning whether to believe their president's views.

A world without natural disasters could mean the world we live in would look completely different to how it does now and many people would have another chance to live. With there being natural disasters in America happening every few months, this is leading the country towards a dystopian feeling world, because it's hard for people to cope with a changing world. When people's lives have changed from their norm without them being able to control it or stop it from happening, people will take matters into their own hands and take control of others.

Changes in people's own worlds are hard enough to deal with for some in America, especially now those who came into the country with family are being separated as if they neither belong in the country than with their own family. The control the government of America has can instantly cause conflict if they wanted to. President Trump has openly conflicted with Kim Jong Un over social media for everyone across the world to see and worry about.

The Movie Outburst

Extract of a short film by Shayla Heywood-Abano

EXT. CINEMA, EARLY AFTERNOON
Three brother; JASON (14), JUNAID (7) and JAY (3) are hanging around outside the CINEMA. They are waiting for their film to start for JASON'S birthday.
JUNAID
Why do we have to watch Peppa pig movie? It your birthday, you're 15 now so that mean we can watch the new Purge movie.

JASON
Just because I am 15 does not mean we can watch whatever we want and anyway JAY would be scared and you to young plus look how excited he is.
JAY
PEPPA PIG, GEORGY PIG, MUMMY PIG, DADDY PIG!
JASON
Come on let's go buy Peppa tickets
JUNAID
I think I will just sit out here and talk to some hot babes

JASON
If you come I will buy you butter popcorn
JUNAID
Okay but you are ruining my street cred
JASON
You're 7! you have no street cred!
JAY
Come! Come! PEPPA!
INT. The boys go and pay for some tickets.

TICKET ATTENDER
What movie would you boys like to see today?
JAY
Peppa please
TICKET ATTENDER
One teenager, one young boy and one toddler mmm £40 please
JASON
WHAT!I was told £10 for one teenage, £6 for kids between 7 and 10 year old and toddlers go free
TICKET ATTENDER
Nope that was yesterday's deal
JASON
Oh I only have £30 sorry Jay no Peppa
JAY

No Peppa
INT. JUNAID pull his brother from the tickets booth
JUNAID
Where did you get that money?
JASON
Alcoholic uncle Sam
JUNAID
He going to kill you when he finds out...

Title card: Little did they know how true that would turn out to be...
END.

Pain

By Sinel Hussein

We say we don't like the feeling
Of being ill
Or over a fall
And when we get an injection or a cut
even if your hand was broken.

We also say we hate diseases
with a passion
but if we can't feel pain
We won't be able to feel the positive feelings like

Being surprised
Being proud you have a life
Happy to have the family you have or even feeling enjoyment
If we couldn't feel pain, we wouldn't be able to feel the good emotions
The world would be the same every day
Humans would turn into robots
because you didn't want to feel a dash of pain
so now there's no feeling
Instead of wishing to have no pain start being happy you have feelings
because without pain there's no positives.

And here we are in 2020 – it's funny how I could predict a world gone wrong
because of all of that is now happening. All I can see is black and white; a grey
sky, an empty road, people walking in sync, no birds flying in the sky, no pets,
no-one even talking to each other. There is no communication, not even a smile
on a face and that's how I knew something had gone wrong. But if I had told
them something was wrong no-one would care because this was "normal" to
them now. It's too late.

Gangs

By Trevon Bryan

What a negative word
Young kids are addicted to drugs before they know their ABCs
Young kids are used by elders
At least I'm still strong
But taking someone's life is wrong

Guns are not fun
It has to be done
Imagine you took someone's son
They wouldn't have time to run

Drugs money isn't your money
Make your money legally

In the pit of their stomachs, full force, but you knew
How tattered horizons give way to something new
For all this started with an envy that did grew
And a jealousy of passion that in your mind did brew

What do you get from drug's money?
When you got arrested the something illegal
Start to do something right
We'll help you fight

On Women Being Judged Only On Their Looks

Inspired by *Only Ever Yours* by Louise O'Neill
By Martha Cabral

This is wrong because
women are only judged on the way they look and not by their personality and
kindness.

This is not right because
if the woman is rude and doesn't have a good personality the men will just use
the women just for the way they look.

This is also wrong because

women want to be loved for who they are on the inside and out.

Men don't appreciate women for who they are on the inside and only appreciate them for the outside.

Some men care about appearance and if they look nice they will talk to you and they don't know your personality yet.

This is wrong.

Speech against Video Games

By Kamarle Wallace

Video games have taken over people's minds, making people miss education and opportunities for life. People even are getting kicked out of schools for attendance for missing so much every day.

There's new things for games every day; new updates, new content, there's no chance of these humble kids getting off these video games any time soon. Kids brainwashed, addicted to these games. Some young kids wanting to start YouTube channels, taking a big risk to drop out of school, and throw their valuable lives away.

Mothers and Fathers spending lots of many just to buy kids games to sit on it the next morning, also not knowing or appreciating the reality of life education and family comes first: NOT GAMES.

I Want

By Deborah Martens

I don't want to be a footballer
I don't want to be a dancer
I don't want to be normal
I don't want to follow people
I don't want to fit in

I want to be noticed for my good and not bad
I want to be someone when I'm older
I want to be who my success leads me to be
I want to be unique
I want to be a leader
I want to be known across for my success
I want to be me.

Fire

By Thomas Lieu

Start from blue turn to yellow, orange then red
Heat increasing, burning and destroying
Many powerful touch will end world life

An uncontrollable beast melting his cage setting free
Letting the anger out and destroying ours home
It is like a bomb exploding straight away
How can we dominate this beast with the sun's life source?
It is making us afraid
                    Scared
                    Terrified
Many of life are lost every year due to fire that breaks out of it cage
How can we stop this?
What will you do?

The Storm

A play by Kirsty Dumfeh

KIRSTY: The storm is getting nearer
OLIVIA: Stay hidden, stay safe
SHARNA: I want to take a closer look...
KEZIAH: No Sharna, its dangerous out there. Do NOT leave the bunker
DIXIE: I hope mum and dad are ok. We should have never run away from home!
KEZIAH: Let me give them a call...* 3 second pause* No signal
KIRSTY: Oh no... the storm could have gotten them already!
OLIVIA: NO! do NOT say that! They are fine, be positive.
SHARNA: The storm is getting nearer; we need to evacuate!
DIXIE: Where are we anyways?
KIRSTY: Check Google Maps
KEZIAH: No signal, stupid.
KIRSTY: Ok, calm down. What do we do then?
SHARNA: let's just explore the area.
KEZIAH: It's not safe, it's not worth it.
SHARNA: Don't be a chicken. I'm leaving
KIRSTY: Im not staying with you, you will lead us to trouble, I'm going with Sharna
DIXIE: Me too.
KEZIAH: I'm warning you
SHARNA: (mockery voice) I'm warning you.*laughter*

RUNS OFF

OLIVIA: I'm worried for them
KEZIAH: I'm not, it's their life decisions,

KIRSTY, DIXIE AND SHARNA'S PERSPECTIVE

DIXIE: WOW, it sure is foggy
KIRSTY: I know right, maybe we should have stayed with KEZIAH AND OLIVIA.
SHARNA: Are you guys chicken 'in out ALREADY?!
KIRSTY: NO, not at all, let's find some shelter.
DIXIE: How about underneath that tree? There is a blackberry bush right next to it.
SHARNA: Not many blackberries on it though.
KIRSTY: I wonder who could have eaten them
SHARNA: Oh look, there's a little hut over there let's explore it.
DIXIE: Who could be in there?
KIRSTY: it looks old and empty from the outside...
DIXIE: Whoever could be in there I do not want to meet them.
SHARNA: Come on guys let's check it out

enters house

SHARNA: HELLOOO?!
KIRSTY: Ssshhhhh! Don't let them here you!
DIXIE: Who's "them"?
KIRSTY: I read this article about a year ago about this hut, there is a man, a man with no eyes, an old man, who hunts down children.
DIXIE: So the skulls on the wall... are not fake?!
SHARNA: That is... AWESOME!!!
DIXIE: NO it isn't! I'm leaving this place... the door is locked what are we going to do?!

KEZIAH AND OLIVIA'S PERSPECTIVE

OLIVIA: I wonder where they are...
KEZIAH: I don't know and I don't care.
OLIVIA: I'm going to find them; you can't ignore them forever just because SHARNA mocked you
KEZIAH: They are probably dead already *mutters under breath* hopefully.
OLIVIA: I heard that...
KEZIAH: *Sarcastically* Heard what? Anyways... meet me here if you don't find them. I'm going to bed.

SHARNA, DIXIE AND KIRSTY'S PERSPECTIVE

DIXIE: WHAT ARE WE GONNA DO?! I'm not living in here forever.

MAN ENTERS BEHIND THEM...

KIRSTY: We are NOT living in here forever, that article I read about the old man is probably fake...
MAN: Fake huh?!
SHARNA: don't bother looking behind you, just run.
MAN: Run where?
DIXIE: WHAT DO YOU WANT FROM US?!
MAN: Your body.
KIRSTY: PLEASE LET US GO! We will find a sacrifice for you.
MAN: You have 24 hours... otherwise I WILL find you.
SHARNA: Thank you sir!
DIXIE: Quick guys! Let's go

LEAVES HOUSE

SHARNA: What the-
DIXIE: What just happened?
KIRSTY: Where are we?
DIXIE: I think we just travelled through time...
SHARNA: AWESOME!
KIRSTY: Its late. Let's fine somewhere to sleep.
DIXIE: We could use those leaves over there as blankets
SHARNA: Smart thinking.

Almost a Haiku

By Harry Tautz

In Maranello

Cars are built.

Good cars, HYPER cars.

Power of Love

By Dima Semir and Muna Barrow

It goes from hellos to good night texts
From hugs to kisses
From like to love
Knowing you're the only one I care about,
is everything
But in the end,
It means nothing
Because you're no longer with me

Issues with tech

By Hector Leon

Nowadays people really depend on their phones. They take over our life making us lazier and less productive as they distract us from our responsibilities. Smartphones have also created new addictions and phobias like being scared that your phone will turn off. Many phone manufacturers have taken over the world and will not stop doing so.

Modern society is really ignorant as they don't know what actually is happening behind the perfect phone. To start with the environmental effect is massive as the plastic and metal need to be extracted using different methods that will release gases contributing to Global Warming. Also the waste management is poor as all the garbage goes underneath the ground making it a waste land, nothing will be able to plant anything there for a couple of thousand years.

The fact that people don't know any of this makes society really naïve as not only phones use technology but also weapons do. All the nuclear tests carried out will affect people and the planet, places like North Korea carry out nuclear tests really frequently.

Flowers

By Mumia Douse-Bah

Flowers consume the nectar of Aphrodite
As they are as beautiful as she.
Their beauty is incomparable for they are the
Originators of life.
Flowers are immortalised angels in which
 We feed.
They may be alluring and innocent
And yet possess the power of a fallen angel
For life can be consumed
By a flower.

Life

By Mumia Douse-Bah

For death is a luxury and life is restrictive,
The only birds may be our own demise
Science may be concise and complex but the limitation is life
The conundrum that is life.
Like cattle, we are driven to money
For it is a promise of life
As money is but a piece of paper
Constructed from a means of life.
For the beings that may seem omnipotent
Seemingly sit powerless.
 Beliefs are a quandary for they may lead nowhere
For life is pure
But living is tainted.

Perfection

By Niven Marimootoo

Perfection is my enemy.
It always gets the best of me,
Saying who I should and shouldn't be.
Perfection will be the death of me,
Always infecting me,
Messing with my mentality.
They say keep your enemies closer,
Maybe I shouldn't have listened.
I have kept it so close,
Now my enemy is me.

Hard to Obtain and Easily Taken

By Jasmine Robinson

Where are you most powerful?
Your home?
Well, sure you do what want, control your own space
But you're only powerful because that's where you stay
Its where you live. Yes
Is it yours? No
So is it really your power
Who's to say
No one

No one really has power
We are all condemned by boundaries
Boundaries that are made to keep us in place
But what place?
Is it the place that gives people power?
Or is it the person who gives the place a reputation
A reputation that can give or take power

Power takes time to build, like your home
There will always time when power is weak unstable and vulnerable,
like you
So are you the power
Who knows...

Money

By Goodness Odubanjo

Everyone desires fortune.
But for money is nothing but paper
Always on the go to spend money
Well remember this honey
Money can't buy you respect
But how people speak of it
Is not how it seems.
Time is more valuable than money
You can get more money
But cannot get more time in life
So enjoy life to the fullest.

What is the World?

By Havana Parish and Cheyenne Daley

The world is a mysterious place, full of powers
From which is made of hours.
The world is a ball of fire
Which suits everyone's desire.
The world is a war zone, full of hatred
Where dangerous things can be created.
The world is the circle of life
When a faithful man loves his wife.
The world is a rich man's life
Until his days are numbered,
Everyone beneath him shall be slumbered.

Prologue

By Bella Burton

Two families born of different races
Both failing to see God's great creations
Perfect imperfection in this nation
They battle for love yet full of hatred
Yellow, blue and red against red and white
Sharing many things in common, hidden by their spite
Battling for success in the evening and night
The world is watching, hoping to win this fight
The match of Colombia and England last night...

ELLEN WILKINSON

Home, Sweet, Home

By Kimberly Gonsalves

Home is where my heart is locked and secured
Out taking challenging adventures
Morning is the start of a new day on a cooling breeze.
Excitement and laughter we have together

Sweet melody of music coming from the singing birds.
Wishing I was part of them
Every memory always stays right here.
Enjoying my life peaceful like a swimming Swan
This is my place of power

Happiness is where you feel comfortable.
Our heart stays safe
My family and I are a group of adorable ducks
Every day my house feels like a home.

Home

By Seterah Shamloo

Home is a place of comfort.
Home is a place of Happiness.
I can be as free as a beautiful bird at home.
Home, oh, sweet, home!
I can be powerful, when I'm at home.

Family is Love

By Anonymous J

Family loves you for who you are.
As lucky as you can be to have a family,
Make a change, make them proud.
I promise, you will see a difference.
Like the sun going down
You are safe in their hands.

City

By Eleftheria Siadima

I am at the airport
Everything is different
And I panic! Shh, that's what I hear.
With my parents, but I don't feel safe,

But there, there she comes!
The amazing Anna, to pick us up
We are off to her house
When we arrive I see my cous,
I am so happy!

I have a good time
Going through Germany
I now feel safe!

But, it's time to guy
I have to leave
I'll see them again
I promise...

I'm nobody

By Anonymous A.S

I'm nobody,
I am a lanky lazy human being,
But with my brain I can be as big as I wanna be,

I can live my dream,
I can be who I wanna,
And BOOM living my dream.

My brain,
My soul,
My heart,
My shame,
Are the only things that are left of me!

Home – Family

By Krisha Damania

Happiness lays in my home.
Of all the troubles, I went through my family was there to make me feel safe and secure.
My friends and family wrap me up in their euphoria.
Elders are there to show you the right path. Without them you can't be anyone.

Famiy is there to support you, love you and take care of you.
Always remember them,
My friends and family bring me joy, oh I'm ecstatic, elated.
I'm gleeful at thought of them.
Love that they have given to us can never be forgetful.
You push me to be successful.

ELTHAM HILL

Place of power

By Alicia Su

A place of power
A place of happiness
A place of freedom

The outrageous world around me
All I think of
Emotions, powerful adjectives, similes
This is the world around me
Literature, techniques, structure
All I think of
Writing poems, anything

The power of freedom
Frees me, makes me think wildly
It's like I'm anywhere around the
World.
Happiness brings me love
The power of happiness and love
Makes me feel vivid

This is my place of power.

Wonder

By Gabriela Melani

Sometimes I wonder...
I wonder if the curtains are tired of covering our secrets,
I wonder if the pillows are complaining about the tears we drown them in,
I wonder if the cupboard can really hold all our skeletons,
I wonder if the door can handle all the secrets trying to get out.

Then I wonder that, if one day, they won't have to worry about that.
Because they'll be no one to cry on the pillows,
and no one to shut the door,
and no one to pull the curtains.

Far, Far Away

By Liberty Nichols O'Connell

Up in the North,
Far, Far away.
There is a place of Magic and Wonder.
A place of Passion and Love,
Far, Far away.

I drift away and all my worries are solved
I fade away and no thoughts pester me,
I get whisked away into another universe,
Somewhere that is just mine,
Somewhere that I can be me,
No one else but me,
Just me far, far away.

In this place I am not crazy, but creative,
Not hated, but loved.
In this place, I am far, far away.

Where the angels go to rest,
Where souls are set free,
This place I call heaven.

Found

By May Thomson

A few steps into the forest,
You are no longer their property,
Not without your consent,
They can tie you down,
They can chain you up,
But they cannot contain your mind,
Your beautiful mind they'll hate because it's not their own,
Because your singular light out-shines theirs collectively,
You are safe beyond the fence,
The place where the land isn't theirs,
Here, you can live without any restraint,
You are welcome here, lost girl.
Take a seat, a bed of grass and moss,
Let the branches grow around your wrists,
Do not be alarmed.
You have found us now.

The Place of Love

By Ellie Kinch

The place you escape to,
the place you feel right,
the feeling everyone wants,
the feeling of love.

When the mood gives, you joy,
when that someone is there,
when nothing can hurt you,
love makes it right.

The butterflies in your stomach,
the feeling of your heart beating swiftly,
the rush when the world runs so fast,
when your heart makes the world.

This place is inside of you,
and yet all around,
this is the place you escape to,
and everyone wants that love.

Treehouse

By Abigail Obeyisi

It's just a bunch of twigs and sticks,
strung up and tied down pathetically.
It's just a bit of nature's own,
taken out of humanity's soul.
It's just a tad of guiltiness,
as I break down trees repeatedly.
But there's no one to hear,
no one to see,
that these very same branches comfort me.
So, it is mine and that's all I have to say
and you can never ever take it away.

Writing

By Connie Johnson

A place of beauty
a place to escape to when life is dark.
A place where light shines bright
and a place of love, hope and joy.
A place of power.

The ink runs from my soul
carrying cooped up thoughts,
the happy, the sad, and the ones that haunt.
This is my place of power.

Once a blank piece of paper,
now a scroll filled with flowing words.
Words that blossom when read,
words that make up my place of power.

A portal to a world,
a world free from war and violence,
a world of mystery,
a world I call my place of power.

With You

By Ela Salih

With you I laugh even when I want to cry,
if I would have to live without you, I would
Die, with you I want to remain, every night
and day, with you I feel loved, may
my life stay this way.

With you I know I can breathe.
Life is not the same.
With you nothing matters.
With you the moon glows brighter.
This, I hope you know,
With you there are many,
Reasons why you make me glow.

With you my heart celebrates and sings.

Just knowing that you're my mum,
makes me feel things.
With you my happiness persists,
through good and bad seasons,
by your side with many reasons.

Escape

By Emily North

Everything I saw,
right there,
right now,
was beautiful.

I read about it,
I thought about it,
and I made it a reality.

I left my life behind.

My hated,
Bullied,
And hurt,
Life.
To be free.

I am still the same person,
in the same hated world,
but you can escape to another world.

But only if you knew how,
to find your place of escape.

EVELINA HOSPITAL

The Beach

By MJ, year 6

Before
Round and edgy
Plain and dull
They sit there like a ball
Waiting to roll...

The rain is falling like shattering glass
With the smell of seaweed passing by
I am tracing the past
 of the footsteps I made last.

Next thing I know I hear seagulls squawking
I stop for a minute and as I get soaked
My cousin walks out
Do we have bright or dull ahead of us both?

After
But there is one thing I like
And I do it when the sun is shining bright
Running down the rocky steps

To the tree house where my tabby last slept
But I find her on the swing
Lying in the afternoon sun.

Now there's cushions and snacks
I had a nap
All my friends come running more and more
They woke me up with the slam of the new oak door.

The Park

By JU, year 8

Now

Rubbish lies asleep.
Swear words are scratched onto paint,
The park is empty.

It's scary quiet.
Taste of rotten bananas,
Yucky smells of dirt.

The park holds a chill.
Annoying pigeons invade,
It is out of place.

New

The rubbish has gone.
Escaped from vandalism,
The park is happy.

Salted caramel.
Lovely smells of fresh cut grass,
You can hear laughter.

The park holds a warmth.
Children take over,
The park is happy.

A recipe for a full loud and alive library

By JU, year 8

When I walked into the old library, I could smell its old dusty scent. The taste of bitter lemon filled my mouth. Just with the smell and taste I could tell this was not a fun place. I could see computers taking over and invading the home of the books. This huge area was filled with tables. There were few shelves and not many books. I had been to this place before. It had been filled with people and shouting and laughing. But now it was empty. No one was here. It was silent. Empty. Dead.

Ingredients:
A glug of new books
A handful of people
A pinch of colour
A spoonful of thyme
A sprinkle of time
A peck of lavender
A mixture of sweet smells
A cupful chocolate

Method:
Pre-heat the oven to 30 degrees.
Brush a glug of new books onto the shelves.
Mix in a handful of happy people until the mix is bursting with laughter.
Throw in a spoonful of thyme.
Drop a sprinkle of time to the mixture.
Stir in a peck of lavender.
Whisk in a mixture of sweet smells until the mixture smells sweet.
Knead your cupful of chocolate into the mix so that it tastes delicious.
Sieve a pinch of colour over the mixed ingredients.
Put the prepared mixture into the oven for 10 minutes.
When your mixture has finished cooking, take out of the oven and sprinkle over your library of choice.

The New Library:

As I walked closer to the doors of the library I thought that they were going to fly open and explode with laughter. I opened the doors and a mixture of sweet smells flew out. I could taste sweet chocolate. I could see walls and walls filled with brand new books. People everywhere were talking, laughing and smiling. It seemed to be the happiest place ever. This was the only library that anyone thought felt alive.

A Coliseum Stone

By LA, Year 8

One day there was a stone in the coliseum. It was rolling around the rough coliseum floor. It decided one day that it wanted to go and visit the people, because it was feeling lonely.

So it rolled down the steps of the coliseum and could smell the humidity of Italy, like iron from the sea.

When it got outside the people screamed and ran away, which made the rock feel lonely and sad. The rock thought about all the things it had seen, like Roman gladiator fights, changes over time, tourists coming to visit and now there is just stone and fences.

The sad stone rolled back into the coliseum and thought of all the memories and they made him happy. It fell asleep for another two thousand years.

My day as a family oven

By SR, Year 3

It looks like my family are coming from the airport today because a note on the fridge said family coming today. I'm so excited, but I'm so dirty and filthy. I should start cleaning myself.

Scrub scrub scrub!

Yay! I'm shiny and clean and ready to cook.

Knock knock

Oh no they're early. Luckily I've got a super speed button so I can finish cleaning the yucky dirt and now I will make my invisible hands come out to open the door.

My family come in, drop their bags and say hello. My family look happy but exhausted and hungry. Let's start making food!

I turn myself on and I start feeling all warm and cosy inside. First, I cook the chips. I put them inside myself with my long stretchy, squishy hands. They turn crispy and brown. Next, I put in the sweet honey chicken. It smells so delicious I start to dribble. The chicken turns crispy like the chips and I put some masala on it.

Ding ding

It's ready! Time to open the door of the oven and take out the chicken and chips. I think my family are going to love the chicken and chips I've made.

Mum opens my door and takes out the food. The children come running in.

Mum goes into the living room and puts the food on a picnic blanket. They all sit on the toshak, eat the scrumptious food with their hands and put on traditional Afghani music.

The lonely roller-coaster

By OS, Year 6

The roller-coaster was sitting in the darkness waiting to be reopened. As he was waiting for the children to climb on his seats he watched the man slowly push the button for him to rapidly move on the track. He felt nervous as he was going higher and higher. When the sharp and steep drop was about to fall he could hear the music screaming in his face, then that is when he started to fall down the track. The wind blowing hard in his face as if he could not breathe. As soon as he hit the bottom, he could smell the oily food drop on his seats. He could also smell the mould on his wheels as they made a weird noise. He was being hit by branches and eating them, it tasted horrible as if he had eaten poop. Also, he had swallowed some leaves which really did not taste of anything. He was half way through before he broke down. He could feel the children and adults panicking and touching and banging on him. He felt sad and lonely for no one could understand him. He needed a friend. He did not like that children abused him, he wished that he could just run away and never come back.

The Annoyed Slide

By NR, Year 5

Luring my eye was the twisty slide catching up on the latest gossip .
The slide was being snatched into a trance by the sweet smell of
Sizzling sausages and accidentally touched the inside of a boys nostril
Picking out snot because the boy was rapidly sliding down it.
Disgustedly the slide shook its body to get off the snot like a slithery snake.
The boy fell flat on his face, flooding the ground with tears.
"That's what you get!" yelled the slide.
The boy ran off.
"And don't come back!!!" it yelled again. Ffinally there was peace and
Quiet.
Until a chubby adult came sliding down –
"Who is this heavy child? Yikes it's a grownup!"
Swallowing the human the slide tasted the bitter taste of deodorant...

The sacred tree

By MJ, Year 6

One day there was a normal tree in a normal wood. Last summer I loved all the children climbing on me, being able to feel their soft palms on my rough branches and long windy trunk. Hearing them laugh was the best part, all their emotions just popped out of nowhere. But one day it started raining, all the children fled from the wood. I was all lonely once again. Seeing the rain is the worst part, feeling it slowly trickle down my me. It was all cold. I thought to myself, I am never to see children again. Until one day... Three joyful youngsters came on the trot constantly until they passed me. One of them stopped and shouted back to the others,
"HEY wait there here's a good tree for the tree house!"
That shocked me. "TREE HOUSE" I shouted. Oops, I thought to myself.
"What was that?" shouted one of the children.

A Day in the Life of Winnie

By MC, Year 6

Hi I'm Winnie
I am a Maltese puppy
I am 15 weeks old
I love my brother Jensen.
This morning I woke up at 6am. That may seem early to you but to me I like to wake up early and start the as early as possible so that I can spend as much time as possible with my mummy.
Me and mummy always play together, and we always play with my favourite toy Mr Wriggle, then I may get up to mischief by climbing up the stairs, that I have not learnt.

Disneyland

By FP, Year 2

I went to Disneyland in Paris with mum and dad
Happy
Big dresses
Loud music
Bees buzzing
Princesses
Colourful

Do not turn off the lights.

By BKP Year 1

Once there was a boy, his name was Daniel and every time he went to school he walked past a mental asylum which was abandoned.

Every time he walked past his hair would stand up on his neck as he was petrified.

One day he made the last mistake of his life.

He went into the asylum to explore; stupidly he crept in alone...

As he passed the front door, he was exposed to the electric chairs and barbed wires.

Voices of the victims came through the wall asking for help.

His spine tingled and his blood went cold.

There was a light in the electric chair room shining into the bloodied clothes hanging from the ceiling.

He looked down and the person's skeleton was on the floor chained up.

Daniel heard footsteps coming from upstairs shouting GET OUT OF MY HOUSE or DIE.

Daniel thought it was the winds, but suddenly a dark figure started to approach him very slowly.

Daniel heard a high pitch scream and never saw the day light again.

Emily's new bunny

By EW Year 3

Once upon a time there was a girl called Emily. She was going to get a new pet bunny. She bought it a cage and some food. She called the bunny Sophie. She was feeling really excited. The bunny's fur was really soft, and her bedroom smelled like strawberries and blossom. She could see the sky and the sun and buildings through her window, and she could hear the birds and the washing machine from downstairs. The excitement tasted spicy.

When her bunny arrived Emily ran down the stairs to open the door to get her bunny. Her bunny's fur was white with brown patches. She named her bunny Millie, she put her in her cage and fed her and gave her some water. Made her a nice comfy bed out of some hay. Before bed she took Millie out of her cage and went to the shops to buy her some toys and some more food and take her to the vets to get her checked. Then they went home and played in Emily's bedroom for 10 minutes before bed time. Then she put her back in the cage, and tucked her into her nice comfy bed. They both went to sleep.

In the morning Emily's friends came round and Emily showed them her new bunny Millie. They all played with Millie all afternoon.

The End

Four Friends

By MJ, Year 6

It was 5am in the morning; a young girl woke up with a loud yawn. She heard a knock on the door. She looked out of her window and three of her friends were impatiently standing outside her door. She checked what time it was, and screamed "IT IS 5 AM". She slid her small, petite feet into her fluffy white slippers, and answered the door in quick form. Three of her friends ran through the door and almost flattened her. Yet she was in her pyjamas and all three of her friends were ready dressed and had eaten breakfast.

"Hi" shouted Zofia with an untoasted hot cross bun in her mouth.

"Shush" shouted Milla, "my mum is still asleep".

The heard a clatter coming from the stairs "hide" shouted Coco quickly.

"It's only my cat," said Milla softly. Sparkle meowed. Crumble slowly walked out of Millas' room with his head down and started scratching her leg; Milla instantly knew there was something wrong. She turned around and looked towards her bedroom her window was open.

Dannie gasped and sarcastically yelled "woooow someone broke into your house."

In a stern voice Coco said, "This is serious, I noticed something missing from Milla's room."

"What," Milla replied quickly;

"Crumbles collar is missing off his side table" said Coco.

"It's probably in the drawer," said Dannie in a relaxed tone.

Milla rushed into her room and checked if it was there, it was not. Suddenly Sparkle started searching the floor, Milla then knew there had been another animal in the house. Out of nowhere, Sparkle sniffed out a white feather from Crumbles bed.

"It all makes sense, your window is open, and Crumble's collar is missing, there was a white feather in his bed and Crumble is acting weird," said Zofia whilst summing up all the clues.

"That's it," shouted Dannie "we've got all the clues, remember Milla; you told me that Crumble goes all tipsy when a wild bird has been in the house."

"Well, there is a white feather" said Coco, "obviously a bird feather, and there are loads of seagulls outside".

Joy

By AS, Year 8

If you could feel joy it would feel warm and refreshing,
If you could smell joy it would smell aromatic and fragrant,
If you could hear joy it would sound like children playing and laughing,
If you could taste joy it would taste sweet and delicious,
If you could see joy it would look like people having fun and spending time together.

If joy was a place it would be the beach!

Lowry the dog

By BKP, Year 1

Once upon a time, there was a dog-called Lowry. He went to the park and he had a ball, which played with on his own for a while. Then he found friend called Rosie. Rosie played with him in the park and then Lowry made another friend called Eddie. All three played together because they are nice dogs, it was a play-fighting game. The park had a green slide and red swings, Lowry had many friends at the park who he played with. The grass and trees were covered in yellow and white flowers. It was very windy and the grass, flowers and leaves on the trees were moving from side to side. I was in the park and I threw the ball to them, I was happy.

FOREST HILL SCHOOL

MY PLACE OF POWER

A collection of pieces based on the themes of place and power.

Men of The Triremes

By James Casey

With a great thud the sterns of the ships crash against the eastern sands. The masts of the Achaean triremes stand tall; dancing in the winds that flow out of the valley of Troy. Colours flow across the wood of the ships, like the morning dew rolls down the hills, presenting the pale hues of the high grass and flowers. On the adorned ships lie steadfast soldiers from far west. Bravest among them is the master runner; his divine origins show in the fearless stare Achilles pushes upon the men of troy and the mountains alike. He and his fellow warriors pace themselves: to accept death, if not of themselves, then of the glorious men they travelled so far with.

Feet are light on the decks; ready to make great lunges in an instant. Priests walk end-to-end on the ships making prayers to the gods, who would be friend or foe in this war just as much as any soldier, general or king. And as Achilles' flowing hair paraded in the sea air he drew a great sword from his side; it was clean for now but would soon be stained red with many a Trojan.

Fate was now set, and no feat of man could direct its flow. The first signs of Hector's company appeared over the horizon. Hearts raced. Great commands were bellowed and men poured onto the beaches on mass. What would be their bloody fate?

The Clock Outside

By James Casey

Never have I met as deep a sleeper as me. Armadas could fire their whole arsenal over me and I would not come any closer to ending my slumber. But that night, on the hour every hour, the harsh chimes would tune from the tower, seemingly erected only to serve as a towering evil to those who wish to sleep in Cork City. A bane to comfy nights and sweet dreams.

When the sky had been blanketed with cloudy night and the city dwellers had decided that the day had been made, the tower would protest this decision and in cruel retaliation would undo whatever progress the sleepers had made towards reaching dreamy unconsciousness, and I was among this disturbed, sleep-impoverished mob. On one night I woke early in expectation of the sonorous militia that crawl through every street and eardrum of those in its sphere of influence. I could see the monument from my window and as I rested my tired gaze on the tower and waited as my fate approached, I had grown into submission of its audio autocracy. I was powerless; an attempt to reach sleep would be futile. All I could do was wait for the clock outside to chime.

Iceland

By Alexander Kemmeni

The sky cracked like a whip
spews of searing magma seeped out like blood in a cut
Lava trickling down the face of the bleeding mountain
Ruptures of acidic gas swept through the sky

Thunder beat through the sky like drums
Lightning strummed like a guitar
The world turning to an ocean of fire
As the old world was set ablaze

In the distance, a sleeping giant arose
creeping through valleys, shaping the earth
The Glacier an ancient beast that formed the land and tore through it once more
The glacier that battles the volcano in a battle to the death with people trapped between

Fire and Ice
Fire and Ice

The stage was set

By Tylan Thomas

The stage was set. A match against the team who were top of the league above us, while we struggled for form in our league. It was a fairytale match-up. Whether it be on a professional level, or Sunday league, the feeling doesn't change.Tthe nerves still kick in and the adrenaline still pumps. Being the underdog is never easy, but being the favourite isn't either. I don't know what it was like to be the favourite in that situation, but I know that MY head was all over the place.

The car journey felt like it was going on forever. Seconds felt like minutes, minutes felt like hours. Nothing could take my mind off of the match-up ahead. The prospect of a cup semi-final doesn't come around every day, or every season. Even just as we were leaving, my heart was pounding, fighting like an angry gorilla trying to get out of its cage. It is crazy to think that the two possible outcomes could leave you in completely different states of mind after: sensational, overflowing joy or drowning, depressing sadness.

I have to admit that, although being captain, I was not entirely confident about the game ahead. As I sat there paralysed by the thoughts of what could be on the other side of the car journey, multiple outcomes continued to circulate around my head. Would we win or would we lose? Who knew at that point? All we knew was who were favourites and I think that you can guess who that was.

As I stepped out of the car, the nerves hit me like a brick wall. It was as if I had been in a twelve round boxing match. My legs were like jelly, my throat had become bone dry to the point in which I could not speak and a knockout blow of nerves made me immensely dizzy.

Trying to get my head focused was as hard as trying to find a needle in a haystack. After multiple, over exaggerated breaths I managed to compose myself enough to get started on the warm up. After an intense warm up, my muscles had eased and I became less tense. I stepped up to the centre circle as I do every game, shook the opposing captains and referees' hands, and did the coin toss. For the first time in what seemed like an eternity, I won the toss. This little event of fortune made me just wonder if the outcome of this match could be different to what I had imagined.

As the game started, fate really decided to give a blow to my hope, with us going down after just a few minutes. The opposition were lions, hunting down whoever had the ball in packs. I felt powerless. We were more scared about conceding again than playing football. But then, after a lucky break our striker slotted the ball into the goal as cool as ice. My belief was back. After the restart, all of the fear was gone. The lions had become passengers, watching us play around them. Our football was flowing as smoothly as a river. This was until about a minute before half time, when they scored again. Maybe our fairy tale underdog beating giant fantasy wouldn't come true. The feel at half time was depressing. Everyone sat and listened to the manager in silence, bewildered about what had just happened on the pitch. I had totally zoned out during the team talk but he must have said something truly inspirational, because as much as the rest of the team was inspired, he managed to inspire my soul. I stepped onto the pitch with confidence beaming on my face and power in every stride that I took. The team talk had certainly worked because almost immediately, we scored. A floated free kick came in over the top as I made a darting run in behind to slot home our second goal. The joy was more contained this time as we were not looking to go behind for a third time this match. The rest of the match was cagey. Both teams were too scared to attack. Everyone was drained of energy. Then, as went into the few minutes of added time I made a break forward and received a crunching challenge on the edge of the box. It was as if he had used all of his remaining energy to lunge himself at me. I stayed on the floor for a second, trying to catch my breath. As I rose, I realised where I was, I had practised this more times than I could count. I knew this was mine.

One of the strikers asked to take the kick; I just fixed my eyes on him and indicated that this was my free kick, my chance, my opportunity, and he trotted on. As I took my three steps back as I do every time, about one hundred different emotions flooded my brain. I glanced a look up at the sky and I knew what I was going to do. It was as if the heavens had spoken to me. I was on the left hand side of the penalty box, and I gave the top right hand corner of the goal a deep stare. I was in my place of power. When the ref blew the whistle, what I saw when I glanced up in the sky was about to become a reality. I took my three steps towards the ball and struck the ball as sweet as a nut. I felt like the ball was in the air for an eternity. I felt like I could see each individual spin on the ball. I felt the ball hit the back of the net. A ROAR exploded out of me! I could not believe it. It went exactly how I had pictured it when I took that glance up to the heavens. The lion in my chest which was fighting to get out had finally exploded out and had broken free. As I was dog piled by my team mates, even they could not contain this beast which was overflowing with joy.

Thankfully, the feeling after the match was not a drowning, depressing sadness, but was the sensational, overflowing joy which I had prayed for before the match.

We did win the match. We did get our fairy tale ending.

Lost dreams, lost lives

By Tylan Thomas

I was just having a normal walk home, taking in the beautiful night sky while recollecting the amazing night which I had just had. The stars were shining bright, bright like the future of many of those in the tower. I took a quick glance down at my phone to see if that girl had messaged me. She had left the party before me and lived in the tower. I looked up in disappointment and saw it ablaze.

I rushed to the tower, adrenaline pumping through my body as fast as the fire was spreading. The flames were engulfing the tower, and all that could be heard were tortured screams coming from an already tortured building. It took me a minute to refocus. My phone buzzed, making me realize what I had to do. I typed in nine-nine-nine as fast as I could, my hands shaking with anxiety and nerve. When I got through to the fire service, I couldn't speak. A mix of scorching heat frightening nerves had made my throat bone dry. I managed to explain to the operator what was happening, with tears in my eyes and a wobble in my voice. By the time I had got off of the phone, the flame had doubled in size. Then it clicked in my head. The girl! Will she make it through?

Mountain Ruler

By Abdullahi Siad

It was my 12th birthday and we went mountain climbing. It was my mom, my sister and I, and I was the most athletic. As I was climbing in the hot weather of Vegas, I could feel the powerful sun's raging flames hit me in my back. Then for a moment, I stopped to look behind me and saw the only source of life for miles around. It was Vegas and it was such a beautiful sight.
I got to the top not long after. Then looking behind me again, it was so exotic to see life where you never imagine it happening. As I was standing strong, tall and powerful, I felt mighty. As the people of Vegas looked defenceless I said "Respect the mighty Abdi that rules the mountains." From now on I feel power at every mountain I go to.

The place where I felt powerful

By Reece Stennett

I spend the days, hours, minutes, seconds of waiting anxiously to go to Surrey Quays cinema. The feeling of walking into the building is overwhelming. As soon as you walk in through the doors there is a massive projector showing all the movies that are going to be shown. I always have that warm feeling when I walk into the cinema. The journey towards the cinema is always excruciating. We take one train to Surrey Quays, and it's about a five minute walk until you actually get to the cinema. The walk towards the cinema always feels so long, especially if you are going to see a movie that you have been waiting to see for ages.

When we finally get to the cinema there is always the smell of popcorn and hotdogs coming through the kitchen in the cinema. We walk towards the counter and pay for the tickets. One thing that I don't like about Surrey Quays is that it's always so expensive and sometimes they raise the prices. Whereas, if you go to Peckham cinema they will give you tickets for a very cheap price. So when we buy our tickets, we get sent to a person who checks our them and tells us what screen to go to. As we walk down the corridor towards the screen we were told to go to, my brother and I always look at the pictures of films that are coming to the cinema soon and debate which movie we are going to watch next.

As we walk into the cinema there is always a warm comforting feeling as you see the big 10 foot screen playing 20 minutes worth of adverts. As you turn the corner facing the seats you are met by another wall of the smell of popcorn. I always feel invincible when I walk into the cinema- I feel like the world's a much happier place. And when there are lots of people in the cinema, it feels like we are one

WINDRUSH STORIES

A collection of poems based on work completed at the British Library's exhibition of Windrush: Songs in a Strange Land.

New Land

By Qaalid Omar

I worked as a chef back in Jamaica.
I'm at a riot in Brixton.
We need to fight against discrimination.
Flames. lots and lots of flames.
The sky filled with smoke.
Loud screaming and banging.
Fired up but the fact the police are fighting me has me alert.
Virtually everything seems to be floating.
All I ask is for Britain to treat us not as animals but instead with respect.
The British are head strong and it feels almost nebulous to get the respect I dream of.

Cultures are getting in the way of one another

By Reece Stennett

My heart and soul goes into everything I do. I am a famous campaigner who is fighting for world peace; I will not go to my death bed with knowing I didn't bring world peace.
The streets of Piccadilly Circus are crowding with people fighting for world peace, the florescent colours from the posters are blinding me.
My fellow campaigners march alongside me chanting "Bring us together!!" it feels like we are singing sings that are begging for freedom.
People are standing tall and proud, a mixture of backgrounds brought together.
The honking of horns and the chants from people feels influential.
I can feel freedom.
I feel like the smells of people determination are overwhelming.
When I sleep I dream of being on a beach, while knowing that everyone around the world has come together.
At this point I want food to cure my hunger from walking up and down all day.
Cultures are getting in the way of one another.

New places

By Tylan Thomas

Joshua Bailey is my name, and I have come from Jamaica with a feeling of freedom.
I am now in England, at the port of Dover, mesmerised by the beautiful view.
I am here to work, and if required, struggle and grind to make a good life for myself.
As I arrived at the docks, I could see the beautiful view of the English coastline.
I can hear the sea gulls calling,
And I am bewildered by the large amount of noise pollution from the masses of people which is invading my ears.
I can feel the ice cold sea breeze battering me and making me shiver,
I also keep bumping into people as I try to hustle myself off of the boat.
I have a feeling of prosperity and overconfidence as I step off of the boat.
I dream of my future being as bright as the sun back home in Jamaica.
I dream of having a carefree life where I can live without economic fears.
I would like to make enough money so that I can send home money as my family are poor.
Something that may stop me from doing these things is racial inequality.
It is unfair that I should miss out on my dreams because of the colour of my skin.

Origins
Our group was inspired by learning about the Windrush Generation. This is a collection of pieces based upon the pupils' own family tales of origin.

Fighting in the cities

By Alexander Kemmeni

Fighting in the cities, fighting in the air, fighting in the seas, fighting everywhere,
Tearing nations apart without care.
A never ending war machine rolling over resistance, rolling over anyone that wasn't one of theirs,
Splitting continents apart in these few short years.

One of these fledging nations tried resisting evil,
Yet abandoned and betrayed by old allies.
Resisting would be futile and cause needless warfare,
This was the beginning of a new world order where the Germans ruled everywhere.

Some tried to escape, some tried to fight back, yet many were too scared,
Civilians left to starve as the Nazis did not care.
A man and women had nothing left for them apart from their dreams,
And two children the mother bears.

Yet they persevered and held on till the end,
Building up a family at the war's end.
The family and children hurt and damaged,
But they would live on and raise generations to come.

An evil was defeated,
And hope had finally come.

WHAT HE SAW

A collection of pieces inspired by the story of Daedalus and Icarus. The writing imagines what Icarus saw as he flew too close to the sun.

I wonder what he saw

By Reece Stennett

The muffled words of "don't fly to close to the sun" flew through my ears.
The higher I got, the more freedom I felt,
The freedom took over, it was too late to stop.
One, two, three... my mind started to freeze,
The tiny little feathers falling into the sea.
I flapped and flapped and flapped but struggling did not come to my pleasure,
The harder I tried the lower I fell.
The two seconds of freedom felt like a distant memory, as the sun begun to fade,
I began to see my reflection in the sea, death was upon me.
I screamed and yelled and screamed again, but no one was coming to my praise,
My father yelled but I did not care, I knew it was far too late .
SPLASH! Went the water, darkness filled my brain,
I took one last look at the sun, and away with my pain...

I am feeling free. I am feeling powerful.

By Tylan Thomas

I am pumping my arms and I am soaring through the sky. A feeling of hubris is flowing through me. The sea breeze is gently blowing against me. The beautiful view of the deep blue ocean is the full canvas which I am heavily engulfed in. I am feeling free. I am feeling powerful. I am feeling on top of the world. As I take a glance up at the blazing sun, I take a moment to take in the warming heat. I hear my father calling to me, but I do not listen. I look into the light blue sky which looks as smooth and soft as velvet. I am beginning to pump my wings harder and harder. Overconfidence is fuelling my arms as I rocket through the sky. I hear my father calling again, but I do not listen once again. I reach the peak of which my arms won't flap any longer. The muscles in my arms are now burning as hot as the sun, my fuel has run out. I look back up and the clouds look like angels, angels about to wave away my life...

HAMPSTEAD SCHOOL

Year 7 and 8 pieces

This Location is my Destination

By Paris Omer

The TV was as big as two strong, beefy men. It also had a glossy background which was 30 inch tall, that when I come home I can watch Netflix on it. The clock was round and always moved its second hand smoothly, sucking up every second of the day. The sofa felt as soft as a thousand pillows mixed up with a million feathers. The exercise bike was as tall as eight chairs stacked up together, with pedals that go as fast as Usain Bolt's skinny, long legs. The smooth, silky wall is so creamy that if you feel it, it will feel like you are touching E45. The floor beneath the carpet was so cold that every time I come home, I'm walking on the sky of Antarctica.

You could hear the sounds of people who are drunk at the bar swearing until they fall over and faint. The trollies rattled as workers from Tesco pushed them. There were gangsters in the alleyway listening to music on tiny speakers. The cosy smell of KFC swirled up my nose like a slow tornado. The posh, bright chandelier hanged above my head clinging together like a million crystals. This location is my destination.

Spanglish

By Kaya DuCasse

Her mouth moved,
Foreign words forming on the tip of her tongue,
She spoke rapid fire,
Mixing both Spanish and English,
Not quite gibberish,
Where she spoke with her hands,
Not quite fluent in a language
You had to speak it to understand it,
Spoken so fast,
All that is seen is her tongue flickering,
Where movements expressed your words,
And Kitchen and Chicken all sounded the same,
Never spoke just one language,
But all three,
It all sounded so sweet to me,
Never judged the way she liked to speak,
It was all the same,
She spoke with power,
To dominate every word,
To blow you away,
Never had nothing to say,
Unspoken words in a language you wouldn't dare to say,
Stories of the past clearest in the strangest ways,
Complaining about Enchiladas,
Shouting at adverts,
Saying words wouldn't stop us,
Mixing languages,
Lost in rapid fire,
Lost yet found,
Understanding,
Yet not understanding why she's ranting,
Spanglish we call it,
Not a fluent language,
Not complete English or Spanish,
Spanglish.
Understand the language.

Sometimes

By Kaya DuCasse

"So what do you do?
Sometimes I play this game,
Sometimes I stare out of the window,
Wondering what it'd be like to be all the same,
Or I just gaze at the ceiling,
Sometimes I do nothing at all,
What else do I have to do except stall,
Sometimes I finish this story on my laptop,
Sometimes I stare at a blank piece of paper,
The blank represents my thoughts,
Empty and small not long and not too short.

Home

By Mohammad Rayan Dianalan

This is a place to relax
A place where you pay your tax.
A place that keeps shelter over your head
And stays with you for the life ahead.

This is a place that stays strong like a fortress
When the worst become worse.
This is a place that everyone has
A place that you see after school or work
So a house is a delightful sight.

A house is a place where love lives
A place where memories come to exist
We stay indoors almost 24/7
And how it should be
Because a house is all we need.

Troubled Questions

By Lana Matkovic

I wonder about these unanswered questions I have,
that dance around my mind every day,
like how we think as we act.
Does it all depend on your mood?
Maybe the weather impacts your thinking?
Or just the thought of reality kills your expectations.
Is reality really the most intimidating?

When I'm in the fresh breeze taking a break,
from the harsh world in my beach house in southern Europe,
it's peaceful. Beautiful. Mesmerising- it's perfection.
I completely zone out and forget about all of my troubles.
Why I hold it dear to my heart:
it's moments full of contentment and bliss;
the breath-taking views from balconies,
the azure sky showered with contrasting embellishments,
the crystallised sea compliments it all.
It's my lifeline; addictive but not poisonous.
So does it mean that the place we're in affects our happiness?

When I go there I only think about myself,
what I want, what I want to do.
What's bad about being selfish?

Back home, I have to comprehend that people are the cause of others' deaths,
and it deeply scares me.
On the other hand, people often care more for others than themselves;
being careful of what is said and done to not offend anyone.
But when least expected, the person you love and care about will immensely hurt you.
When we involve ourselves in other people's lives, can we justify our actions?
Should we go through life placidly but ignorantly?

Does ignorance provide true prosperity?

Therefore I think;
is there such a thing as a perfect life?

The Park

By Yasir Ahmed

A place where your worries will drift away
Where you can be yourself and have a nice day
This location is pure open space
Where you can see children running around in a race
Most of your view will be emerald green
You can see people kicking about in a football team
This location is an element of nature.
Very safe and barely any danger
This location is very important to me.
Where no one can judge you and you can be free!

My idea of a perfect world.

By Anas Faris

This is a place where I feel drawn to,
Where I go when things get tough,
When I can't handle what life throws at me,
Or when reality hits you hard in the face.

It's a place where I wonder off to,
When I'm feeling sad, lonely,
Or when I need to get away from the real world,
It's like a drug but it's not harmful: it's addictive,
It makes me feel worthy of living another day.

It's got everything I've ever dreamed of,
From a breath-taking view,
To a whole lifetime of relaxation,
The Maya blue sky glistening every second of the day,
The fresh breeze brushing against my face,
The vivacious palm trees giving life to nature,
The bright blue sea shining before my very eyes.

It's a place that's a part of my soul,
Is it wrong for me to be selfish?
Is it society's fault?
Maybe it is, maybe it isn't,
Maybe it's the fact that people care more about themselves than others.

Its beauty cannot be comprehended by your mind,
It's where my heart exhales,
I just zone out and contemplate why life has come to what it is,
That would be my ideal. Perfect. World.

But it's not...

The bedroom

By Amir Hussain

This is a place of rest
This is a place which is the best
This is a place where there is no other
All there is, is you and your brother

This is your location
Because this is where you can express your emotion
This is a place where you're the spectator
This is where you're the creator

This is a place which has a view
This is a place which has no queue
This is a place to sleep
This is a place to keep

Money

By Subhan Hussain

Money is something everyone wants
It can also buy you lunch.
Money can buy you many things
You could get a car or a jar of honey.

Money is precious, Money is power.
Money is a devil looking to devour
Money is our lord
on which we dedicate every breath.

Money is a sword
which will cut us at the first chance.
Money can buy you many things
But Happiness.

YEAR 9 AND 10 PIECES

A simple place

By Maya Moreau

The ambient wind hums a low dull whistle, as spears of sentiment nip at each hair.
On this very hill I rest alone,
Overlooking all the worries that lie below.

Finally, silence.

As the sun sets I revel in what's left,
A moment dear in my heart from which i will never part.
A still place of serenity,
Will I ever get there?

My powerful Place

By Aafreen Ahmed

The place which embodies all the power I need,
Is not your typical 'place'.
The place where I feel powerful is in my own flesh and blood,
My body is my own and it is filled with layers of plush clouds,
Coloured with a sweet tone of caramel.
My body is the scent of freshly brewed coffee,
Caffeinated like the powerful heaven it is.
My body is unique place,
Not shared or changed by the physicality of man.
It is my powerful place and empowers me every day,
To be the beacon of hope
I know I am.

Between these two covers

By Batul Chebab

Gingerly, you open the leather-bound book, stroking the spine which was cracked as a result of the countless times it had been read back-to-front. An aroma of printed ink and pressed pages cloud your senses, inviting you to revisit the classic. The pad of your thumb slides across the crumpled paper. Orderly letters stood in perfect rows, shoulder-to-shoulder, clad in identical font uniforms. Despite their rigid looks, each character joins with the next to form words that crafted world with limitless bounds. To an onlooker the act seems like a simple movement, but with each turn of the page you get pulled further in. A gateway to time travel across eras or warping through time and space. Eyes flit over dog-eared pages, desperately swallowing every sentence; clinging to every word. A universe of knowledge and experiences held within the confines of two covers.

Destroyer of Humanity...

By Hanna Tariku

Power. Those who possess this have the ability to manipulate people's thoughts and feelings. They are able to move people emotionally, mentally and physically. People strive for this luxury. For many, it's wanted more than money. It makes people go mad, tempts them to betray their family and friends, urges them to commit bad deeds. A beast waiting to have full control of its owner. On many occasions it creates war between countries; and between the heart and the mind.

Power makes people blind towards everyone but themselves. Power is the destroyer of humanity.

Power

By Diogo Lino-Luz

Power is strength,
Power is the strength that we give ourselves,
Our self-esteem and our courage to stand up for what is right,
Power is often a good thing,
However, Power can make us bad,
It can make us turn evil and disobey our morals,
And make us engage in nonsense quarrels,
Power is what we make it out to be,
From global superpower to girl power,
Power is a word,
And it's a word that changes its appearance.

Home

By Diogo Lino-Luz

Home,
A place of love,
A place of tender,
A place that no other can replicate,
A place of comfort,
A place of love,
A place of relaxation and family fun,
I imagine entering my warm, comforting, luxurious home,
With the smell of my mum's beef ruggedly cooking in a pan,
I can imagine my pearly white, relaxing sofa,
And I can imagine the fine, quilted blanked landing on me,
I can feel the love and hugs from my family,
I can feel,
Home.

The Island

By Diogo Lino-Luz

A beautiful, vivacious and open island pops out of the purple and crystal blue horizon. The island is full of wonder and full of life as far as the eye can see. The bright lights simmer in the crystal blue tone set by the all-seeing horizon. The interesting and wonderful contrast between the vivid and pitch black colours create a sense of beauty and paints the image into my soul like a canvas. The setting feeds into my soul and cannot be detached.
Even when cold doubts,
And plans go awry.

The War of Adaptability

By Zahra Baidani

We enter. One by one. Filing in silently. We feel as if a chunk of our lives has been bitten of by the monster we call school. Swirled in a mixture of depression, stress, anger, denial. Swallowed with a gulp of homework, tests, criticism, comparison. At our darkest moment we are churned in a mixture of all these combined. Some are crushed in the heaviness of it all, turning to means beyond their allowed accessibility. Then we are spat out. And now. Our feelings numbed. Centre ID's to hide all individualism. These next hours, we are constantly reminded, will be the determining factors for the rest of our lives. An impact to be felt by ourselves and all those who surround us. Too many succumb to the pressures.
But not I.

The ticking of the clock binds us closer and closer. Every passing second brings not the usual feelings of dread, regret, anger. Instead excitement courses through my veins. Years of bottled up understanding and preparation to be tested in this final battle of knowledge. As we take our assigned seats, the hall as quiet as the darkest moments before dawn, I look around me and see nothing but a sea of fear and panic, etched deeply into the frowns and sighs of those for whom it is too late. And yet for me, this is the epitome of my place of.

Power.

"The Speech He Gives"

By Venera Mulla

She wakes up every morning, her rubbles of roof and remnants of her buffet stuck to her mind she lays down her life to protect the ones she loves, he does the same. They cling to their children, the tinnitus of their minds ringing; she begs not to pick up. He stands up from the murky grey-like shadows and sees the sea of red around him, he begs for land. The little girl cries as she clings to her parched voice as cries elevate the forgotten land. Together, they are lost and alone. "We are here faced by fascists. Not just their calculating brutality but their belief that they are superior."

She cries tears that will never be silenced, she screams for her love as he lays buried beneath all the layers that completed his hell. The ceaseless inferno of grey. The children will never see light like they wish to have seen before, they will not know the swings that our own children do, they will not laugh or giggle, for forever in their minds will be set this memory, this loss so great it burns our earth to the ground. So great our humanity cries, much like them. "We know they must be defeated". So, at night they sleep on the mistakes of our own.

Whereas, he ties his suit together, the cameras flash brightly, he plans another attack, it isn't his loss. Besides he must fight the monster, those whom are so powerful they face a threat to him. His daughter hums quietly, her hands clinging to the metals of the swing, she sways back and forth. The red ribbon in her hair flows away, it spins, before it flies to the stormy, upcoming skies.

Why?

Rajiyah Ahmed

From sources of religions to sources of literature
The fine, weathered page of a writer's life
The haste shoving into school bags, to the
doe eyed girls with unshed tears flipping the last page
From such wonders of Austen to the dramatics of 'peare'
The musty odour of a worn page, small and flat these worlds remain,
peopled only by the blackened words left there
as we travel from whirlwind romances to the depths of the obsolete darkness.
Only to fall from wuthering heights into the clutches of Big Brother.
Yet it is brought to life as our eyes spark alight to travel into the tale of another
Only then do we wonder
Do we surrender ourselves to the words of others?

Death Cup

By Batoul Mayahi

Everybody should be treated the same,
No conflict and no pain,
I hear screams of children,
In the building left hidden,
Laughter of evil men,
When are you going to see time and again?

Women left abused shrieking,
When is the army seeking?
Shoved in, where is the helping?
I'm right here, witnessing them yelping,
My mind so full of misery,
But what about the ones with severe injury?

My heart pounding feels like it's gonna melt,
The fire raging was the only thing I smelt,
So when are you going to stand up...
Before the world becomes a death cup.

Dreams

By Marmarie Zaloom

As the stars twinkle and sparkle all that's left to do is enjoy a lengthy slumber. And that time finally comes. Clambering up the stairs, each step making legs feel weaker and weaker and then finally you collapse into your bed. That luxurious feeling of your pillow plushing against your face and your mattress adjusting to your body. Your socket to recharge. By every blink your eyelids get heavier and heavier and you're out. Unconscious. Your soul escapes and you suddenly you start to enrol into a new world. The world of your dreams. A series of thoughts, images and sensations drift into your head. You are unconsciously in charge; even though you are half dead. Embarking on adventures and being chased by dark mysterious silhouettes. But when you start to adjust to the situation, golden rays of sunlight illuminate your face. A new day. But you struggle to remember.

ROUGH SOUL

By Athian Akec

The fabric of time was lost, weighed down by heavy syncopated beats; rhythms that were the gospel of movement. Rhythms that would teach your body to move, to move without fear or hesitation but with pure soul. Hamurkn1 was the greatest drummer of the day, with nothing but his drums he would reprogram the air, bending those listening to his will. It was said once a naive dancer had ventured blindly into tumultuous thunder of the New Sogal dancehall, forced by the intense rhythms into a trance so strong they forgot themselves - leaving with a rough soul and broken arms.

The walls were jet black – their darkness endlessly expansive. Amongst the sea of Black faces lay one White mask. The drummer stood firm, commanding and controlling the pace of his beats with a subtle arrogance, moving only his experience laden hands. The rhythm was the yam of the people – in those days it was said the man who does not value yam over his life does not value his life at all. In that room one could not see; one could only feel. Hamurkn staggered drunkenly - the only one in the room whose movements were not eclipsed by the trance of the drummer's rhythm - with his knife tucked into his side. Still free, Hamurkn's hands began to follow the rhythm. Soulfully, but enigmatically his hands flowed in an unusual way. The rhythm was as intoxicating as the palm wine he had hours before – but only on his hands, the rest of his body remained drunk, uncoordinated. He staggered forward, each step tumultuously uncoordinated towards the drummer, with a suturing anger deep in his eyes. Blinded by the darkness, and the trance of the rhythm, his hand gripped the knife and plunged it into the heart of the drummer. This naïve dancer was Hamurkn.

Before the madness had erupted one man remained uncoordinated, almost as though he was uninvited by the rhythm, that man was the son of the British coronal tasked with managing the western section of the British Empire. When he had first arrived, he caught malaria. The only being with medicine powerful to cure him was the daughter of the king. Since the day she had cured him he had thrown himself into culture of the people his father had travelled thousands of miles to civilise. Traveling for hours to partake in the rhythm of the native people. When the ear-piercing panic began he was the first one to leave.

The air of the room grew thick and weighted; breathing became an almost impossible task. This was not because of some physical sensation, but because of a collective sense of shock – striking deep into the hearts of those present. This day had only been talked of in hushed proverbs, by men with unwise tongues. It was once said, that the day the drummer fell at the hands of a knife, that it was the day the ancestors where to have their wrath. Blue bats fell from the wall as they walked in, both taking apprehensive reserved steps. What separated him from the rest was his gun, held not as an act of power but as an act of fear. His expression was tainted with a sense of regret. He shouted an inaudible command in the direction of Hamurkn – receiving no reply he advanced towards him. With regret seeping into his voice his commanded "a na-ejide gị maka ọnwụ nke onye na-egwu egwu egwu nmmu" - you are under arrest for the death of the legendary drummer nmmu.

The King's court was flooded, not with the water of the river but, with people. Starck dejected faces hung in the air, like the last words of an obituary. Faces that stung. Stung of greif and anguish. As the king emerged the court fell into silence. The flute sounded with a blue tone, notes that were detracted but focused. The notes hung in the air dissonantly, reminiscent of a dream formed of weird mismatching shapes. As the king first spoke the notes dissipated into the water laden air. It was said that Hamnkurn was lost, lost behind the bars of the British. The king said "the custom of our people is that once every one hundred years the village drummer will fall in an act of great violence. The ancestors speak in proverbs not words. Their wished cannot always be understood by the living.", the crowd was astonished by his words. He muttered "the heart of the British is cooled by the ice of western Europe if they violate our customs as they have their buildings will be burnt so they can feel the warmth of our gleaming sun.".

*Hamurkn is the surname of the famous pan Africanist president Ghana Kwame Nkrumah reversed

HARLINGTON SCHOOL

Streets of Holland

By Sabrina Ali

Strolling down the street
And I smell the sweet smell
Of fresh pancakes.

Strolling down the street
And I hear the crowd
Greeting each other
"goede morgen"

Strolling down the street
And I feel the warm breeze
On my face.

Strolling down the street
And I see beauty all around
Me.

Strolling down the streets
Of Holland.

My Mother

By Hany Zouargui

My mother dear, my love for you is strong,
You're where I belong.

Filled with love and care,
Always ready to share,
I love you with all my heart,
You're smart,
Giving orders,
Taking questions,
You are beautiful.

Your eyes are smoky quartz glistening in the sun,
Your brown hair tied in a bun,
Your skin as white as snow,
You give me a funky flow.

You carried me as a baby,
Safely am I with you.

You're my special place,
I love you Mum.

My Last Day in Italy

13th February 2013 – 11:37 am
I got my last hug.

12:00 pm (midday)
I taste my salty tears dripping down my face.

12:02 pm
I can hear muffled voices urging me on.

12:03 pm
It feels like I'm underwater.

12:19 pm
In my seat.
Thoughts flood my mind.

14th June 2018
Five years have passed, but I will never forget the last hug I got from my best friend. Now I know that there will always be a piece of me in Palermo.

In my eyes Goa is ...

By Liza Rodrigues

In my eyes, Goa is
A beautiful, fair city.

It's just so surprising,
When I step on the sand.

The wind hops around me,
And I start to dance along.

It just feels so amazing,
When I swim under the sea,
And the fish dance with me.

It's a brand new world.

Goa, it's me.

Glory

By: Taran Bolina

Glory:
I'm doing what I want,
Time to stop all the drama,
I live it for the summer,
And nothing is gonna change any faster,
Gonna break some records.

We got time for success,
Time to do it like Curry 9 3's,
One game,
Time for everyone to get ready,
Time is limited.

I'm doing what I want,
Time to stop all the drama,
I live it for the summer,
And nothing is gonna change any faster,
Gonna break some records.

Intense game of Fortnite,
Time to stay online,
One life no respawns,
Don't use your life half way through the game.

Time to play Fortnite,
In my bedroom,
Don't waste my time,
You can't stop this because I'm flying,
Flying higher than Big Shaq,
I'm playing Fortnite all day.

More wins,
More skins,
More credits,
More success.

I'm doing what I want,
Time to stop all the drama,
I live it for the summer,
Live it for the summer,
And nothing is gonna change any faster,
Gonna break some records
Let's live it for the playoffs.

Childhood

By Ayub Mohamed

Sweden is all I think when someone says the word "CHILDHOOD". Also my little brother puking all over my shoes. But why? First reason. The food! Not only is the nutella there more valuable than gold, but if I went to a Swedish restaurant, it will have to close because they were out of food. I and all my siblings were all born in Sweden in town called Rinkeby, Stockholm. This is where all my cousins and aunties and uncles live and we visit nearly every year. And every time we visit for the summer holiday, we go to this amazing amusement park called Gruna Lund (Green land in English).

It is amazing! There are rides which are so scary that some people go home and never want to go back again. There is one ride called free-fall which I managed to go 5 TIMES! It goes up all the way until you can see the whole of Stockholm. And then it goes down to the bottom in 3 seconds. We stayed in our auntie's house where our favourite cousins live. They are all so nice to us. They give us things like food and they let us play with them on their games console. And they play football with us whenever we want. Sometimes, we go to a restaurant and they pay. Now that is nice!

I remember going back to my old home where I was raised. When I went in, everything looked a bit unfamiliar. But then my mum showed me all my old things and pictures. After that I started to remember things like the playground outside and when me and the others played hide and seek outside. Those were my good old days. Anyway, it always is a sad moment when my family have to go back to England. But we always come back the next year.

Coming together as a family is the best thing to do. Brothers, sisters, mother, father and cousins are really important in my life and I am grateful for them being in my life. And you should be grateful too.

East London, My Home

East London may be cold,
East London, full of memories,
But have you lived there?
My childhood.
It's not just a place for me,
It's my home.
East London,
It's my home.
My family, friends are there,
The house is always crazy loud,
We end up shutting the windows,
It's my birth place, my home.

It may have been annoying to move
Around eleven times,
But in ways it's humorous and exciting,
We end up fighting over rooms,

It's where we got our two babies,
They need pillows to sleep on,
Laila and Romeo our two cats.

It's where my mum was born,
My mum is very special to me,
The way she talks is odd.

She made the weirdest names out of my name,
I don't know where she gets them from,
"Sheena", "Shisha" all sorts, but its entertaining,
And brings laughter to us.

LANGLEY PARK SCHOOL FOR GIRLS

The Divide

Scary and lost, left feeling sad and bemused.
Segregated, worried, separated and confused
Scared of what might happen next.
With war at our feet each night I can't sleep
Wondering thinking what next will it be?

With Palestine and Iran were once united
Now divided!
How could this be?
Friends have parted and now it's just me.
"When will we see?" I ask, "How could this be?"
The divide has happened is it a dream or for real?
But then we must get stronger! As powerful as can be.
Our countries, Palestine and Iran
One day we will unite again and operate as one

It is a Cemetery

It is a cemetery. The names, carved on the graves. The flowers, dying of sadness. The birds, singing at the funerals. My Nan and grandad, buried, lying in peace. My aunty, lying next to them in her own, brown coffin. Nan and grandad of the year, was written on their graves. Flowers, yellow, her favourite colour. Flowers, blue, his favourite colour. India, where they came from. Croydon, where they live. I love them. I never met them. Nevertheless, in my heart they are there. It is a cemetery.

My House

My house is where I wait the whole day
to get to, there is no place as comfortable as my
home. Home sweet home!

This place is where you play, rest and ALWAYS
stay yourself! Once you are here you can do
whatever you want and whenever you want.
Home sweet home!

Every place is special but my home is
the most special place for ME! I feel
safe, I'm protected it's just such a safe place!
Home sweet home!

It has this special smell of vanilla! Everyday
I hear this sound but I still can't say
what it is! When I see my dog
coming out of the room I feel so good
I just love it! Home sweet home!

Only Mum

I feel the soft fluff of your jumper,
the words you said to me,
"I will always love you",
the comfort of your knee.

The taste of your cooking never out of my mind,
because I really need you,
and you're super kind.

The one most comfy place to be,
is cuddled in your arms mummy.

Sizzle

Sizzle, sizzle
Pop, pop
Goes the breakfast
Beep, beep
Goes the microwave.

"Hey why won't the TV work?" shouts my grandad who
can't work the TV.
Woof, woof
Goes the dog barking at the post-man.
Vrr, vrr
Goes the kettle.

"Milk or sugar?" calls my nan – who never
remembers.
Clink, clink
Goes the plates.

Then everything goes quiet like a page being
turned in a book. I plop down on the sofa
with a smile. The usual routine is what my
family are like and I love the way they
are.

My favourite place

My favourite place to be
The only place I want to be
This gives me power held within me

All my memories in one
Clasped together
with one lock of the door.
It's the place which will hold forever more.

It's the place where I spend Christmas.
It's the place where I bake.
It's the place where all our birthdays are held.
It's a place called home.

Places I enjoy.
Places that make me feel special.
My family.

The people I have known my entire life.
My mum, my dad, my twin.
A place where I can call home.
A place I have always known.
My family.

My routine, the smells when Dad's cooking,
how mum would be having a cup of tea.
Harry playing his drums, me watching the world go by.
A place where I can call home.
My family.

Books
I own.
In my mum's room
on the book shelf.
The smell.
The feel.
A place I can call home.

All my memories in one
clasped together
with one lock of the door.
It's the place which will hold forever more.

Loving Nan

Smell; as I enter the clean kitchen I can smell the
Chocolate cake rising in the oven. The potatoes roasting on
the fire as we all gather around for a Sunday lunch.

Hear; the sound of laughter and joy as we spend some
family time. Jokes being made as smile come in from
every direction. The ladies having a gossip girl talk while
the men have fun spending time together as one.

See; then a thunderstorm comes. Hearts broken. Tears
emerging from every thought, The strong winds brushing
against the old trees. Apples falling as autumn turns to
winter. The garden becomes a jungle as time passes. No
one to take care of it as our lives move on with a deep
ditch in our souls. The memories of love turn to dust. All
that was once will never be the same again.

She will always be in our hearts.
My Nan.
RIP...

Italy

I wake up in the morning,
shuffled onto the balcony.
Lots of people around the street,
cars beeping and fumes rising.

Spectacular views of mountains opposite,
the sky a soft blue,
clouds like cotton buds.
Excited for the day ahead.

Arriving at the waterpark,
happy shouts and thrilled squeals,
wanting to go in even more than before.

Splash!
Jumped in the water,
as cold as I'd ever been,
swimming to the bottom around people like an obstacle course.

Running to the waterslide,
big and long but I've not changed my mind.
Later on come back so wet,
eating ice-cream that is so yummy.

Sun still shining,
but time to leave,
sad but eager for what happens next.

The Seaside

As the waves whoosh while banging on the
Shore.
The sand running through my hands.
The ships gliding on the horizon.
As sun beams bounce off the sea.

The golden coloured sand spread out
before me.
As the screeching sound of seagulls
filled my ears.
The breeze sweeps across my
face.
This is what I love.

Loving Home

I love my home,
it's warm and cosy.
It's a place I feel free,
A place I can be me.
I can tell the scent of my home
from other people's.
The warm fireplace
and comfy chairs
make me know it's a place where I belong.
Scented candles,
pictures and memories
placed on shelves.
My home may not be perfect,
but it's special to me.
Warm hearts and loving people
who are always here for me no matter what.

My house at Christmas time

Christmas time is the best time

Helping to decorate the tree

Right, put that bauble there

I try to put the star on top

Snow falls and I leave footprints wherever I go

Time to make the Christmas feast

Mum makes mince pies for us to enjoy

And a great big turkey is being prepared

Santa then comes with presents for everyone

The Bookshelf

Shining lights that lead you to a brilliant world.
A world where anything is possible.
A world where the things you love the most surround you.
The smell of the constant perfume of an everyday story to tell.

Pictures, maps and posters of nowadays memories.
Books, diaries and comics full of stories to engage you.
Side to side from the comfy bed right next to the outstanding window.
Reminding you of the outside world.

Flags and maps hanging on the ceiling,
Caught your intentions and dreams for a future.
History, romance, fantasy and comedy books shined from all the others.
They were the sweet top on the shelf.

The dark colours and vibrant senses,
Framed in your mind the image of your future adventures.
The humanity stands out of the frames
That now are memories.

Posters all over the walls make you feel inside the story.
The glossy white paint shines with the sunlight.
All over the room you can see the dreams that my mind brought alive.
This is a place that makes me feel like me and nobody else.

My First House

My first house, the best sight of all,
its sights of the past is what is most emotional of all.
It had brick stairs which led up to a glass door, followed by a
polished wooden glazed door.
It had five bedrooms and a ceiling most important of all,
which had spoken to us all. The iron mark which had left us in awe.
The fridge in the kitchen was double-doored on top of a mahogany
wooden floor. The white pale doors and the dark chocolate looking
chairs were egging you to take a bite. My first house, the best sight of
all.

My first house, the ideal smell of all,
it had a jerk pan which started a misty trail of seasoning, making
everyone wait in awe. The flavour of the curry chicken simmering in

the air making you thirsty for a bite. Handmade coleslaw with the scent of mayonnaise. Fried fish which took your breath away once you smelt the peppering sensation of it. Not to mention the smell of your dad's dirty socks. My first house, the ideal smell of all.

My first house, the most noisy of all,
on pavements dogs barking and losing control,
on the roads learners driving in most directions of them all.
Neighbours arguing most boring of all, follower by their daughters horrible thinking of them all.
Birds humming and singing, squirrels savaging for hibernation, foxes tipping over our bins and leaving a smelly item which was poo. My first house, most noisy of all.

My first house, the most interesting of them all,
like a garden filled with berries to pick, where you would pick out daisies and make them into daisy chains, make as much as you could until no more could fit on your wrist. The sofa had holes which went slightly down, and which beside it had a wooden side table that you would constantly bash your head on, until realising you could have had a pillow. My first house, the most interesting of all.

My first house, the best tastes of all,
the curry chicken scuffled down your mouth whilst asking for more. Handmade coleslaw made indoors having some before the ball. Fried fish made on your dad's grill, then straight onto your plate served with a fresh salad: tomato, lettuce and cucumber. My first house, the ideal smell of it all. My first house, the best tastes of them all.

My Home

By Scarlett Benbow, Year 7

My home is one place I love,
because it has all my favourite stuff.
I can express who I am in my home
and my bedroom. I can do and be
anything in my room. I can dance
which I love, I can sleep which
I have to love, I can be anything I want,
I can be free!

I can't be embarrassed.
I can let out my individual personality.
My home is where I treasure my memories,
my home is where I stay,
it's where I walk home every day.
It's where I get ready, play, time with family,
sleep, eat, chill, have fun.
My home is my everything.

My Special Place

While the hot warm
Fire lingered in the air
And the smell from the
Food surrounded the
House like it was its lair.
Warm and safe drinking
Hot chocolate. Warm and
Cosy under a white fluffy
Blanket while watching
Telly.

Cricket

By Eve Peters, Year 7

As I nervously strolled into my parents room I feared for the worst, I could smell my mum's perfume, which was as sweet as a sweet shop.

I could see my parents staring at me blankly, not giving anything away.

Australia could hear my parents' voices they were so loud, yet mine was as quiet as a mouse.

As they awarded me the shocking news my mum passed me a lime wine-gum, and I popped it in my mouth.

My parents hugged me tightly and closely and I could feel their hands on my back.

Dance

From 9-5 in the dance studio
heel toe, heel toe
arms up, arms down
stretching and stretching
you feel free when you dance
you feel excited

The dance studio is my favourite place
to express
to be free
to dance

Jumping higher
pointing 'til your foot hurts
lift up your leg to the stars
push harder to succeed

When you're angry
when you're sad
or when you're happy,
Dance

My Home

The one place I can truly be myself,
Choose what's on my shelves,
Organise, select, tidy,
Be free, dream, explore and see more,
The key to my heart,
No matter how far I stray I always return,
At the end of the day I always yearn
To come home and feel safe,
Relax and refresh,
Restart and re-energise
Never moves, never leaves,
My home is special to me.

A Beach at Night

At night the beach is calm.
The waves slowly pushing
back and forth against the jagged
rocks. The sea covering my feet
but then disappearing into
the twilight sky.
Sand that covered me
as if my mum was putting me
to sleep, pulling the bed sheets
over me creating a warm
sensation running up my spine.
The ruins of a sandcastle lie
as if it was never there. Its
magnificent beauty not many
can see makes me feel
one with the earth.

At night the beach is calm.
The waves slowly pushing
back and forth against
the jagged rocks. Here
I am again but this time
watching from above,
the view is better. I can
still feel the rough waves
even though I might not
be there. The beach comes with
me following my every step.

My Gym

I have grown in this gym,
Evolved from a mere caterpillar into a fully-fledged butterfly.
Moved from the bottom of the food chain to the top,
I know it like the back of my hand.

The satisfying creak of the equipment,
As I soar,
And the soft pad of my feet
As I land.

I have learnt in this gym,
Crumpled up like a paper ball in pain,
Cried in frustration,
But I got back up.

The vibrations of the floor
As I run.
The rush of adrenaline
As I somersault.

I have lived in this gym,
Smiles etched on our faces,
Shaking like a bowl full of jelly with laughter,
I know it like the back of my hand.

My Special Place

Norman Park is my place to be
It makes me happy
As I feel so free
Stepping out onto the track with the adrenaline
Rushing through me
I am ready to run, run as fast as my legs will carry me

The wind and the rain cannot beat me as blood rushes
Through my veins
My hair flies behind me like a horse's mane
So my head is clear of thoughts, my feet pound the
Track once more
The race is over; my heart beats like a drum
But completely worth it as I had so much fun

Camping at Wishford

You could see the beautiful, blissful sunrise climbing over the hills.
The birds dancing all over the sky.
Countryside as far as the eye could see, smells so delightful.

You could feel the wet, dewy grass at your feet, leaking into
your socks.
A chilling breeze sweeping down your spine, cooling you
instantly.

You could feel the warmth of the dying, orange embers
glowing like glitter.
The night smudged across the sky, twinkling sot-like starts
sprinkled over your head.

Peers exchanging thoughts by a single wave.
The pure, happy giggling from my friends and I.
Winking and whispering in every tent nearby.

I could taste the fresh, freezing morning in my mouth.
The cold sweet morning creeping in, one minute at a time.
This lovely spring morning coming once again.

My Holiday

As I lay there looking at the waves go by
I can see the beautiful sun shining brightly in the sky

Out the corner of my eye I saw a shadow gliding by and
realised that it was the sun reflecting off the sky

I have been having such a lovely time with family and
friends, and thought to myself that I never want this
moment to end.

The sunset started to die down and this amazing
holiday was ending. I am proud to say this has been
one of the best holidays.

My memory of my first time at Hillside Animal Sanctuary

The crunch of the gravel cried out a welcome
And the sudden sweet smell of the horses and
Their fresh hay.
Salty wind stings your lips,
You know you're close to the sea.

Birds swim inside you,
As you jump out from the car.
You reach out to touch the horses' course, muddy fur.
You feel the sun shine through you,
Worries fade away,
Like a faint, fuzzy smudge on a chalkboard.

The vast Norfolk sky
Is a painting on a wall.
Birds sing a welcoming tune to you,
You hear your heart beating,
1...2...3...

That hot, tropical summer,
Fluffy white clouds fly across the sky.
Letting your eyelids close,
You imagine the wonderful day ahead of you.
As you gradually open them,
You feel lighter than ever.

My Place of Power

Bangladesh is my place of power

A place where I am happy

Nothing can worry me

Going to different places

Loving everyone around me
Anything seems possible

Doing whatever I want

Everything makes me happy

Seeing loads of family

Happy as can be

My Room

My room is where I sleep
It's full of random things I keep.
I've stuck many pictures on my wall,
And most people say it's very small.

I always hear the birds tweeting,
And the loud noise of a car beeping.
Fairy lights twinkle in the dark,
Lighting up my room with a spark.

A big collection of teddies, dolls, and stationary galore!
But somehow I'm always collecting more.
Posters, old pictures,
The key to my room.

ORLEANS PARK

The Sea

By Daisy Martyn, 8N

The sea was cool
It was a hot sunny day.
We had nothing to do
While we were away.

I sat there with sally
We sat there together.
We couldn't do much
In the scorching hot weather.

When all hope was lost
Something shifted the sand.
The Cat in The Hat
And he offered a hand.

We just looked and we stared
He adjusted the hat that sat on his head.
He shook off the sand
He stood there and said.

"I know it is hot
And the sun is too sunny
But we can have
Lots of good fun that is funny!"

"I have learnt many new tricks"
He started to smile.
He laughed for a bit
And he laughed for a while.
"Yes many new tricks
you're sure to enjoy.
But first let me show you
My lovely new toy."

Now this wasn't good
It was rather bad.
If our mother found out
She would be mad.

"You can't play any tricks
You shouldn't come near
I have not forgotten
When last you were here."

He looked sort of sad
"Now don't be like that."
He kicked the sand
Did the cat in the hat.

He brought out a box
It was big, it was red.
He opened it up
With a nod of his head

Out something shot
Faster than light.
We shielded our eyes
For the light was too bright.

He stood and watched
The light as it flew.
He brought out a hoop
And the light jumped right through.

"It can perform all kinds of tricks
It is very kind.
No it will not bite
It is so hard to find."

"The reason I kept it
Locked up in a box.
Is because it looks a lot
Like a fox."

Sally and I looked at the fox
"You must take it away.
We simply can't keep it
What will our mother say."

When I said that
He seemed rather sad
Then very slowly
He began to get mad

"You always worry about
what others will do.
But whatever happens
It happens to you."

"Why don't you do
What you think is right?
So why can't you keep
This fox made of light?"

"I'm sorry " I said
"It just can't stay.
For you see
our mother will take it away."

"I see"
Said the cat.
"I see your point"
Said the cat in the hat.

He put out a hand
And in sat the fox.
He bent down
And put it inside the box.

He stood up and turned
And walked away .
That was the last
We would ever be able to play.

I often dream about what would have happened
If I had asked him to stay.
Would we have fun with the fox
What would we have been able to play.

I have not seen him
That annoying cat.
He never returned
That cat in the hat.

The Cat in the Hat Loses It...

By Joshua Dudley, 8N

One day the cat in the hat was lying down in the gleaming sun enjoying the weekend with the magical forest opening out onto the beach. The world he lived in was strange yet beautiful. You would occasionally see a flying turtle going by at 100 miles per hour diving into a pink fluffy cloud where they lived. The cat in the hat also owned his own unicorn that he would ride along the sunny beach every day. The one thing he loved the most but has never done was to ride his own jetpack. He would always see people gracefully piercing through the air watching the sunset over the magical hills of earth. However, beyond this beautiful world there lived the most dangerous creature a man could imagine. No one knows what it looks like because no one has lived to tell them about it. Many people have made up myths to scare people so they will not even think about going beyond the dark, gloomy hills which cast a shadow over the mighty beast ready to pounce on anybody that would attempt to take over his land.

The cat in the hat was on his way back from the beach on his unicorn so he could have some dinner. On his way back he heard some weird noises in the forest. At first he thought it was the trees talking to each other but he realised that they were only awake at night. Suddenly, a creature with two heads launched out at him knocking him off of the unicorn which ran away in fear. The creature was still on the ground so he took his chance to run whilst screaming at the top of his voice "HELP!!!" Nobody responded. The cat in the hat had never had anything to fear before in his life. He was now going to leave that peaceful life behind him. The jetpack stations had just come into sight. He sprinted as fast as he could to them thinking he won't be able to be caught up in the air. He reached out for the jetpack and put it on. His dreams had just come true. However when he was in the air he realised he had no idea how to control it, so he was flying all over the place almost hitting turtles. Suddenly, the two headed monster was right behind him. Just then his right engine exploded. He was twirling, breaking the peaceful silence by his deafening, fearful scream. He shut his eyes in fear so he could not see what was about to happen. He lost his hat whilst hurtling towards the ground at top speed. THUMP...

The cat in the hat woke up dazed and confused. His eyes fully open now creating the picture of the three headed monster making him jump. He tried to run away but it grabbed onto him to quickly saying "don't go all I want is a friend." The cat in the hat responded in a shy way saying "so you just wanted a friend all this time." The monster replied saying "yes." The cat in the hat just remembered what happened and realised he had saved his life. The cat in the hat said "do you want to come over to mine today." The monster who was filled with happiness said "yes" instantly. After that night the cat in the hat's life just got way much better as the monster and him became close friends.

The Eternal Death Yacht

By Liam Nugent, 8N

Andy's family had decided to go on a cruise one day.
So they hopped on their yacht and sailed away.
Andy brought along all of his toys.
But one of these toys was made to destroy.
As they sailed towards the sea,
Jessie's plans came to be.
When Andy was fast asleep,
She crawled onto him without a peep.
When Andy felt her on his arm,
He bobbed his head up in alarm.
Alas, it was too late.
Jessie's fingers in his eyes were his checkmate.
He screamed in pain and Jessie laughed,
in little time his bed became a bloodbath.
The parents came and Jessie ran,
As they reached Andy's room their cries sang.
Jessie crept up in the ventilation shaft above the room.
Straight forward she crept under the moon.
She hopped down onto Father's head,
And down below his heart went dead.
Finally Jessie shot her head Mother's way,
And her new victims tear's ended the day.
She leapt up onto Mother's chest,
and clawed endlessly until there was nothing left.
Afterwards Jessie cleaned up the mess,
And the yacht sailed on to victim next.
So if you ever see a lifeless yacht float your way,
Make sure you turn the other way!!!

Avalanche

By Mae Brand, 8N

The avalanche rumbled into view, a thick black cloud full of boulders and dust, and she spared a look over her shoulder to her comrades. As one, they launched into the endless abyss of rubble, snagging tourists and floating them down to the ground. She alighted onto the ground, lowering the young medic she had been carrying to the ground. That seemed to be the last of them. She let out a sigh of relief, glancing around for the other two. That was when she heard it.

The piercing scream echoed round the mountainside, bouncing around in her head like a ball. *Damn* she though, bolting upright as it repeated, pounding on her eardrums like a wrecking ball. She gathered her strength and vaulted up towards the mountain, directing her course towards the piercing sound.

She hovered just above the noise, searching for an opening in the rock, and her eyes sought out a small cavity, only two feet high. She squeezed through, and tumbled into the obsidian depth of the hollow in the rock. She gazed around, searching for the creator of the screams, but the blackness yielded nothing. She called out, her voice amplifying as it clawed its way down the cave, that seemed to be a lot more than a few feet deep.

Then a light appeared at the end of the tunnel. Blinking to clear the hazing spots in her vision

She launched backwards, straight into the cave wall. Her head snapped back into the rock and the edges of her vision faded, just in time for her to register the rocks tumbling over the hole she had squeezed through.

She came to the intense light of the small ball, that hovered just a few inches above her face. Her hands flew to her face and she scrambled backwards, pushing her back against the wall. It flinched back, bobbing into the would be shadows. Its light blinked rapidly at her, long and sharp flashes, which she recognised as morse code. C-O-M-E. She glared at it, why should she, but, as much as she hated to admit it, she had no other way to go than the passage that the light indicated.

The tunnel was so small at times that she had to get on her hands and knees to go through, but it never closed off into a dead, then after hours of grimy travel, it opened up. Before her was an enormous hollow, miles high and tens of miles across. She gazed around stunned, before her rolled a white beach, with rock pools and shells dotted around. The lapis waters reflected the crystal skies, and palm trees hung low along the side meadows.

She ran towards the water, grinning with glee, and laughed. This was a change from rescuing! She gasped as she caught a flicker of a tail, eyes wide as she realised the top half was human! The mermaids soothing voice rang out, splashing through the water. 'Come on, come swim with us, dive with us!', then she disappeared under the waves.

Her smile vanished, and she coursed through the water, struggling to catch up with the mermaid. She ducked her head under and kicked, only just keeping the girl in view. Her lungs burned and she tunnelled up to the surface, but the mermaid turned, and gazing into its sea green eyes, she realised she didn't care, that she just wanted to follow this girl, that everything would be alright, better then alright.

She felt something brush her hand, and gazed at the girl with the beautiful eyes, now right in front of her. Her vision grew dark, and bubbles escaped from her mouth, but she stared placidly through them, eyes locked on the entrancing creature before her. The mermaid smiled, and tugged her hand, drawing her down to the sea bed. It took her hand and led it towards a towering knot of seaweed. The plant entwined in her, and she welcomed it, feeling proud that she knew this as what the mermaid wanted. It grew up her arm and legs, ensnaring her waist, until it reached her neck, squeezing tighter and tighter.

The mermaid smiled, and drifted away, breaking eye contact. Only then, as the plant bruised her throat, did she finally scream.

Blossom

By Natalie Kan, 8N

Blossom sighed as she hung up another missing poster.

"She's been gone for a month now." Sniffed Blossom as she stared at the poster of her sister, Bubbles.

"Maybe she's just hanging out with some unicorns." Snorted Buttercup.

"That's not the point!" snapped Blossom. "If she were hanging out with *unicorns*, she would have told us where she was going!"

"Fine!" Buttercup groaned. "But you should seriously stop hanging out those posters; they're literally *everywhere*!"

Buttercup and Blossom turned around and the streets were covered in posters. All the walls of buildings had missing posters tuck onto it and some were even overlapping. Shop noticeboards had so many missing posters that none of the other advertisements could be seen.

Buttercup grabbed a stray missing poster as it floated in the wind and shoved it in Blossom's face.

"*See?*" shouted Buttercup. Blossom sighed then took the crumpled up missing poster of her sister.

"You're right; maybe we should start looking for her instead." Replied Blossom. "Where do you think Bubbles would go?"

"I don't know," groaned Buttercup sarcastically. "Anywhere with sweets, chocolate, cute things and fun."

"You're not helping!" snapped Blossom. Blossom adjusted her red bow on her head then stomped off, back to their home. Buttercup rolled her eyes then flew after her sister.

Once they were home, Buttercup sat guiltily on the sofa while Blossom marched into their room with a handful of posters. The TV flashed on and then

Buttercup grinned as her favourite TV show began.

Upstairs, Buttercup rolled her eyes then sat down on her desk and sprawled out the posters. She stared at them for a while and grabbed a crayon to begin making a few more posters until she froze and glared at no one in particular.

"Ugh!" shouted Blossom as she shoved the missing posters off of her desk. "This is hopeless!" Blossom buried her face in her hands and began to cry silent tears. The tears ran down her cheek and then splattered against the smooth wooden table.

"Uh, Blossom?" asked a voice.

"Go away, Buttercup!" snapped Blossom. "Can't you see that I'm emotionally crying about our lost sister?"

"Uh, well, I just thought that you should know that you're being kind of dumb right now." Buttercup yawned.

"Why is that so?" hissed Blossom.

"Well, you've been putting up posters ever since she went missing instead of actually *looking* for clues!" Buttercup told Blossom. Blossom turned around to see Buttercup holding a letter. "And I thought *you* were supposed to be the smart one!"

"Whatever." Grumbled Blossom as she snatched the letter form Buttercup. "*Rude.*" Commented Buttercup, folding her arms.

"Dear my beloved sisters." Blossom read out loud. "I am going to the arcade to win a stuffed unicorn; I will be back by dinner time. Love, Blossom."

"She must have written this the day she went missing." Buttercup concluded. Blossom pretended not to hear and then her eyes widened thoughtfully. She stared at Buttercup and smiled.

"This is a big clue, Buttercup!" Blossom exclaimed. "This letter *must* have been written the day that Bubbles went missing! I'm so smart that I worked that out *all by myself*!"

Buttercup rolled her eyes again and Blossom stuffed the letter in her pocket. "Whatever, let's go to the arcade." Groaned Buttercup. Blossom and Buttercup headed to the arcade, Blossom in the lead. Blossom smiled and her head was high as Buttercup followed miserably behind her.

They halted at the front of the arcade. It's large flashing sigh that read 'Neon Arcade' sparkled in a mixture of different neon colours.

"Look!" Blossom exclaimed, pointing at a claw machine game. "This is the game Bubbles was talking about!"

They both hovered over to the claw machine and then studied it carefully. "Why are we staring at it?" Buttercup commented.

"Because that is what detectives do!" Blossom retorted. Blossom looked upwards and grinned as she spotted a CCTV camera.

Blossom and Buttercup headed into the CCTV room where all screens from all the CCTV cameras could be seen. As they were known as the official crime fighters of the town, they were allowed into the room to solve this mystery.

Blossom sat down on the black leather chair and then clicked on the screen that pointed at the unicorn claw machine. She forwarded the footage backwards until it reached the day that Bubbles went missing.

"Aha!" Blossom cried. "There she is!"

She paused the footage and they stared at their sister, Bubbles, putting in fifty pence into the slot to activate the game.

"Un-pause it!" grunted Buttercup. The footage continued and Bubbles attempted numerous amounts of times to win the unicorn but to her disappointment, she never won the stuffed toy.

"Awe, poor Bubbles!" sighed Blossom sympathetically.

"Why doesn't she just smash the machine?" snapped Buttercup. "Then she could have *all* the stuffed animals!"

Blossom ignored Buttercup and watched as Bubbles was just about to put her last fifty pence into the machine; just then, the coin dropped from her hands and then began to frantically roll in the opposite direction. "My penny!" cried Bubbles as she sprinted after it.

"She went around the corner to the arcade!" Blossom concluded. Blossom and Buttercup darted out of the CCTV room and headed to where Bubbles has just been. They turned around the corner and then spotted three road workers. They had fenced off the area around an open manhole and they were drinking coffee, obviously on a lunch break.

"Excuse me!" Blossom called. The three men stopped their conversation and snapped their attention to Blossom.

'What is it?" grunted one of the men.

"How long have you been working on this road?" asked Blossom.

"For around a month." Replied the second man. "Horrible sewage problem! Just about finished the leaks and repaved the road so that it is as good as new."

"Did you happen to see a short girl come here a month ago?" asked Buttercup. "She has blond hair tied in pigtails and she wears a light blue shirt with a black stripe in the middle of it."

"Yeah, that kid obviously didn't see the roadwork signs. She was chasing a fifty pence coin and it fell down the man hole, she went after it and I never saw her come out." The third man answered.

"Thanks." Blossom replied. She then grabbed Buttercup's hand and then they both began to climb into the sewer. Buttercup rapidly climbed down, not breaking a sweat. However, Blossom gradually climbed down, taking extreme caution with each step. Once they got to the bottom, Buttercup scrunched up her nose at the awful smell.

"Ew! Gross!" groaned Buttercup as she hovered over the sewage. Blossom let out a shriek of happiness once she spotted a bit of torn shirt that was stuck to a pipe.

"It's Bubble's shirt! See, it's blue like hers!" Blossom squealed.

"Cool." Buttercup grunted. Blossom licked the shirt and Buttercup winced in disgust.

"Yeah, this hasn't been washed for around a month." Blossom replied. "Judging by where this shirt was torn, Bubbles went right."

The two of them headed down the sewer and Buttercup constantly groaned about the stench and the mess.

Blossom then halted then stared at the ground where a single penny lay.

"Fifty pence." Whispered Buttercup. "Dibs!" Buttercup darted to the ground and grabbed the money.

"Buttercup! That's was Bubble's money!" Blossom hissed.

"Oh, well it's *mine* now!" sniggered Buttercup.

"You're not taking this seriously!"

"You're taking this *too* seriously!"

"At least I *care* about Bubbles!"

"*I'm* the one that found the letter!"

"What are you two arguing about?" a voice asked. Bubbles and Buttercup turned around to see Bubbles staring at them with a puzzled look.

"Bubbles!" Blossom and Buttercup cried in unison as they both tackled her with a bear hug.

"Where have you been?" asked Blossom.

"With a unicorn!" Bubbles giggled. Buttercup and Blossom gaze each other a look of confusion as Bubbles lead them a little bit deeper into the sewers.

She then halted at an old, rotting blue door. Pushing open the door, Bubbles giggled with excitement as she pointed at a large hairy rat standing on two feet with a party hat on its head.

"A unicorn!" giggled Bubbles. Buttercup scrunched up her nose and Blossom gave the rat a look of pure terror.

"She wouldn't leave me alone!" the rat grunted. "I told her I was a rat, *not a* unicorn!"

Buttercup then gave Blossom a sly look.

"Told you she would be with *unicorns*!" sniggered Buttercup.

Spiderman

By Pippa Gray, 8N

Spiderman looked around the busy streets of New York City. He quickly planned where he was heading and flew off the top of the building as quickly as a comet coming down to Earth. People starred in fear as they saw a strange looking figure flying across the city. Spiderman ignored them and headed for the statue of liberty, he needed to find the suspects. Rain started pouring dramatically, but spiderman didn't care. He continued his mission and noticed two small people, with the same description that he saw before. He headed straight down towards them. They quickly ran as soon as they caught spidermans eyesight. The weather was horrible, but it still didn't stop him from doing what he needed to do. Find the suspects.

He lost sight of them, so Spiderman needed to think of something quickly. How was he going to find them? He thought of where he last saw them and the direction they went so he started from there. People gathered around and screams could be heard from every direction of the city. Police were everywhere to be seen. He needed to go somewhere nobody would be able to capture him. He headed for the empire state building. He sat on the top and looked around himself. Cars headed in random directions, people screamed, people looked all around them, to find Spiderman. But Spiderman needed to find the suspects.

As Spiderman was looking around, he heard a noise behind him. He turned round to see the exact suspect had been looking for. The suspect took out a gun and aimed right at Spiderman's head. Spiderman needed to think of something but stayed calm. He grabbed the suspects neck and pulled him to the floor with power. The suspect scream in fear but still held the large silver gun in his shaking hands. Spiderman snatched the gun from him and held it close to the suspects neck. Spiderman whispered gently in his ear, "say your last words, powerpuff girl." She screamed and the gun shot straight through her head. Spiderman dropped the gun and flew off with confidence swimming around him. Spiderman smiled and went down the the streets, clicked his fingers and changed into a normal man on the streets of New York City. People were panicking saying to each other, "did you hear that explosion?, it sounded like it came from the empire state building." Spiderman laughed to himself as he knew he was never going to get caught.

Harrison's Farm

By Thomas King, 8N

It was a cold, bitter night at Harrison's Farm. Once a secret government research facility, experiments with growth enhancers on the ordinary banana created a super mutated banana/ape hybrid, with incredible intelligence, a new establishing society and the ability to fly thanks to the accidental gene that caused abnormal growth of wings, the facilities now sit long abandoned because of large cuts to the MI6. Gerald, the banana's chosen inheritor to the farm, was flying high, moving rapidly to a meeting on the possibility of gaining extra food for the inhabitants. He was in such a hurry he failed to notice on the horizon the very slight glint of a telescopic lens. He also didn't see the rifle it was mounted on. A steady peel held the trigger delicately, barely breathing to avoid barrel sway. Crack! The sound of a rifle was heard all amongst the glades. Gerald swayed, the sea below him, before crashing loudly into the murky depths. The mysterious murderer took off running, thinking he was unseen. However, the local police, and their main man Isaac, were already there. The ground was thick with mud and little tassels of grass stood out like a tiny oasis on a black, evil desert. The assassin stopped, suddenly, and came face to face with Isaac. He jabbed a quick left hook into the assassin's body before almost being taken off his feet by a powerful uppercut. Reeling, he grabbed his baton and smashed into the face of the killer, hidden by a mask, while bloody teeth fell across the moor. Like lightning, the hook came in however it was just a millisecond to slow. Isaac, with his baton, blocked the well-executed punch before slamming the baton into the flesh of his assailant's stomach to then jerk a knee directly into the face. "Stop, stop" he begged.

"Reveal yourself, murderer" Isaac commanded only to come face to face with Gerald's son. "Why did you do it?"

"Daddy used to torture and abuse Mother and me. It was time to stop."

"..."

"What are you going to do?"

"... Save you. Quick get out of here, before my squad arrives."

The young man speedily hurried out of there, before running out into the sunlight.

Get out of there!

By Amelia Mclauchlan 8S

"Move! Get out from there! Run!", screams a desperate voice of which I don't recognise. Pulled so abruptly from my thoughts, I look around dazed and confused. A pair of large, strong hands grip my shoulders, pulling me to the ground. I spin around to see who it was but before my weak eyes focus, a large blast sends sand soaring into the air and severe vibrations running through the ground beneath us. A thick cloud of fog forms, lining the ground as the sand begins its descent. An intense sizzling noise emerges through the fog as the burning sand comes into contact with our damp skin, leaving small blisters in their absence. My head turns frantically around until the true horror of the past events sinks in.

Although the sand now sleeps calmly, and the dense fog has begun to clear, people lie injured and breathlessly calling for help. Most people were more badly affected by the sand then I was, and are almost unrecognisable due to the damaged caused. Those who are mobile go from person to person, cleaning wounds and reuniting lost babies with their mothers. Those who did not make it are being covered in sheets and organised in lines before being left to rest. I fall to my knees, suddenly noticing the few blisters on my arms; they are not too red and are sparse in numbers. I was so lucky.

Then it comes to me. My rescuer! Powered by this thought, I rise to my feet.

"Remember me?" Comes a mocking tone from behind me. A boy, maybe my age, strides into view. He has jet black hair that lies softly on his forehead above his murky brown eyes. He is average in height and messy in appearance. He raises an eyebrow as a smirk slides onto his face.

"A thank you would be nice," he states.

Taken aback by his confidence, my usually strong, powerful words become tangled in my throat and I have to swallow to free them.

"Thank you", I eventually force out. "Why did you save me?"

"Because I can't take down the monarchy alone, can I?"

Follow Me

By Finlay Turner 8S

Jamie : Follow me!

[The two of them spring to their feet, one after the other, and take off in a ferocious sprint. They both manage to climb over a thin fence — they have escaped. At least for the moment]

Anne: (out of breath) Now follow me. I think I know a safe place.

[Anne leads Jamie down a thin, eerie alleyway. It is made out of rundown bricks and old cement]

Jamie: Anne...why are we down here?

Anne: Trust me Jamie.

Jamie : Okay..

Anne: This way.

[She leads a still traumatized Jamie into one of the houses through a backdoor. She takes him all the way up the two flights of stairs and then pulls back a book case that reveals a secret ladder to the attic. At the top are Anne's friends and relatives who she introduces to Jamie}.

Jamie: What is this place?

Anne: Jamie...... Jamie I'm Jewish. This comes with a lot of persecution and punishment, just for my beliefs. I struggle to think what's happening in the concentration camps as we speak. My religion is part of my identity and these soldiers are trying to change who I am just because we are the easy targets.

Jamie: I had no id-

[Before he can finish, there is a loud crashing outside — the soldiers are back. They are hammering on the door downstairs. Everyone in the attic has frozen with fear. They know that their luck has run out — this is it. Everyone, except Anne who is now shaking with rage.]

Anne: No. No more shall my family and myself live in the shadows, afraid of being caught, afraid of being a Jew. We shouldn't be judged for that.

[Anne collects her diary and her Jewish star necklace and walks out the house with tear filled eyes. She knows what is to come, yet her strong sense of moral intelligence guides her to do the brave thing. Jamie runs down after her as her parents cry out in protest. Outside, Anne shows the fact that she is Jewish to the soldier closest to her. She spits on his shoe to show the lack of respect she is giving and receiving. As she runs away from thix minor crime she is shot in the back.

Jamie stands there in shock as the soldiers barge past him, wondering if she got shot for being Jewish or committing that "crime".

The Train to Rouen

By Flynn Moles 8S

A bird pecked at Roger's window. He pulled back the frame and let the carrier pigeon into his room. The first sign of communication from the resistance in a few months. Roger grabbed the bird's foot, opened the canister and put the message on the floor. After giving the skinny pigeon a scrap of bread, he sent it on its long journey back to the resistance.

The note read "TRAIN TO ROUEN TODAY. 1700." He glanced at his miniscule clock- it read 1640.

He slid his silenced magnum into his waistband and shoved his plastic explosive and grenades into his small pack. As he ran down the rickety staircase, the Jewish man who had risked his life accommodating a wanted resistance member called him into his leisure room. On the table sat document papers, a fake passport, and a bottle of Scotch. The whiskey reminded him of home and the nights spent with his English friends, also in Special Forces. He poured the liquid into jewelled glasses. Roger feverishly drank it. He swept up the documents, and spoke to the Jewish man in a hushed tone.

"God bless you." The man nodded with acknowledgement. Roger Ferguson was going back to England.

The documents the man had given him also included the checkpoints stationed around the main streets. On seeing this map, Roger diverted around the locations and carried on through the back streets. The train station was in sight. His hand instinctively went to his gun when he saw several hostile Germans.

'Don't attract attention! Be inconspicuous', he thought to himself. He joined the long queue of people waiting to get onto the train.

The armed Nazi soldiers were checking people for documents and searching them for weapons. Roger Ferguson only noticed this just as one of the soldiers held out his hand. Roger reluctantly passed them to him. The soldier read them intently. A bead of perspiration crawled down Roger's forehead. The soldier nodded, indicating that he had read them and believed they were genuine. He spoke in horrible French with a strong German accent.

"Bag please Sir."

Roger slung the pack of his back. He hesitated, thinking of what to do. He swung the bag at the soldier's head and heard a sickening crunch. There were cries of alarm from in front of him and behind him. He ran for the nearest building.

Bullets shots whizzed passed his head. He took cover in the ground floor of a disused bakery. He peeked out and shot a Nazi square in the chest, splattering a child in dark crimson blood. He shot another officer who was trying to take cover behind the ticket stand. In the distance, Roger could hear the low rumble of a tank. He could now see a convoy of soldiers, who were heavily armed and already getting cover. He lobbed a grenade at the tank, but it exploded too early, and fatally injured a few unlucky civilians. Trying to run deeper into the bakery, he heard a sound of a window being smashed. In the corner of his eye he spotted the grenade. That dangerous object of death was the last thing he saw. He had tried to get home, but had died trying.

The Worst Event of My Life

By Tilly Miller 8S

I have just experienced the worst event of my life, or possibly even anybody's life. As I am writing this, in front of me is a sight as horrific as hell. As much as I do not want to tell you, this is what happened...

Two days ago, which feels like a lifetime ago, we arrived at our holiday on an eye-capturing island off the coast of East Africa. My two daughters and I came here for a relaxing break away from intense and stressful work. Little did we know it was about to get a lot, lot worse.

We arrived to a breathtaking view, a dormant volcano in the distance. Excitement took over us as we joyfully raced towards the welcoming village. It was just peaceful; the noises of cars engines and planes were not to be heard, it was paradise. The wind whistled as the playful waves happily jumped around. Mountains towered over the pretty houses like guards protecting their kingdom. Jolly birds sung merry songs, keeping everyone gleeful. It was all a magical dream of kindness.

Hours flew by like seconds as we delightedly explored the beautiful area. The kids were incredibly keen to go in the luxurious pool as there were slides and artificial waves making it all the more exciting. I told them that they could go tomorrow, which was the worst, most dreadful decision that I have ever and hopefully will ever make.

The next day approached us and it began better than ever. The sun rose up from the sky, brightening up the morning. Early birds tweeted their tunes as the day began. I sent off my two children to the sparkling water park, as promised. I regret this with my whole heart because of what happened next. As the day went on, I felt the ground rumbling and it was getting warmer, but I stupidly did not think anything of it. Gradually, the rumbles got worse and I looked over my shoulder, through the innocent window to see a cloud. This was not just any cloud — it was no cloud that you would ever want to experience. This was a cloud of ashes. The first thing that hit me was this one thought... my children!

My First Day

By Orla Wynne 8S

Today is my first day at Orleans Park and I am from country no one has heard of. I cannot speak English. When I went through the gates I couldn't understand what anyone was saying - it was like I was an alien who had just come to planet earth. I didn't really know where to go or what to do because no one understood me and I couldn't read any of the door numbers. I was stuck until I heard someone calling my name. She was a teacher. She used Google translate to communicate with me which I did not like because it did not say everything correctly. That worried me and I was nervous about how the rest of the day would be. She took me to my form room which is where I met my new teacher and my classmates. They seemed to not really know what to say to me, so they spoke to me in their language which I did not understand but I could tell that they were speaking to me as if I was five years old. Then the teacher, who had spoken to me using google translate, took me into this room. In the room there was this teacher - a tutor, who the school had hired to teach me English and who my parents had paid for. I spent the whole day there and only went out for break and lunch. I would have much rather stayed inside because I did not know anyone and I could not communicate. I just sat alone on a bench and waited for the bell. I don't know if I want to go to school tomorrow. I can't wait till I can speak English because then I can make friends and go to real lessons.

Golden Plated And Godly Animosity

By Yasmeen Shaker 8S

Humans were the embodiment
of animus and war.
Running away from their problems;
To the back door.
I was their last chance
in the modern era
I was their cloudy
and fossil grey cushion.
Clamouring seas cried in agony.
Their old aegean blues swapped for
Shades of reds:
lipstick,
Mahogany.
I detested them,
They put their faith in mayhem
Forgetting about me
completely.

> Holding each other
> in grubby arms

Guns and armour:
The bloodstained,
Sweaty,
Rust-bronze armour.
The breathing cataclysms were:
Sobbing,
Crying,
Hurting,
Lying,
Ethereal scenery
put on their vehement red dresses
 like the eyes of my lost angels.
Black tones of melancholic apathy.
Calamitous endings will strike soon.
Humankind will never feel remorse
For they are vicious and carved out of stone,
But for what they've become,
They will just feel
more alone.
Dying and greying flowers stayed in playpens.
They put their faith in mayhem

Forgetting about me
completely.

My old divine spirits
Choking on their halos,
Getting drunk on rose water,
Pulling out their fragile teeth.
I want to cuff and clip their repugnant wings.
Darkness desired to save them from me
Darkness is like the edge of the cliff of hope.
Darkness was their light.
I am no longer
omnibenevolent
Though I am still
omnipotent.
Casting waves of blood and wine,
They should have known
Their foolish science.
Darkness held them motherly:
"I will always be here... don't you worry."
I am not sorry.
 The regret of the story of bethlehem
It still follows me
They put their faith in mayhem
They would never let nature be.
Forgetting about me
completely.

Suffering screams and ashes made the Earth smile
Moons cried
For the darkness,
For the peace.
Darkness was officially demolished by rageful lustre
My fantasy has become reality.
Hands of hate rose up to the heavens,
Human skulls simply rotted in the ground
within seconds
People prayed to me...
They should have prayed to darkness.
Submerged
in loving agony
they were
Never happier,
I was a radiant sun.
They put their faith in mayhem
Forgetting about me completely.

The Earth is just a bloodthirsty dress
of vengeance now,
Hung from a broken rack of more beautiful garments.
For it is a shame
That they never realised
Blackness was their true love.
I was the true gloom
I was the source of them being in the doldrums
I was the blue
I was the one who started slavery,
Genocide,
Depression,
And hurt.
I started all suffering.
Thank me for them now being gone.
There are many other worlds destroy and condemn.
They no longer have faith,
Nor memory,
But a creator who abominates them with ardent fury
That will remember all the moral evil and barbaric cruelty
For infinity on high.

Not An Ordinary Coach Ride

By Oliver Ritchie 8S

As my eyes widened, a cold breeze of air blew in my face. I felt the rubble on my arms, leaving imprints as the tiny rocks dug into my skin. Where I was was unknown to me, and where I came from had left nothing more than a scar in my brain. I saw a blurred figure, blocking out all the light, and I felt myself being lifted by strong arms. Not once did I feel the urge struggle - I just lay there, lifeless, defeated.

I opened my eyes, expecting still to be under all that rubble, but instead I was on a bus with people who looked twice as scared and twice as drowsy. I saw a child crying without any care of what people thought of him, which left me wondering what we were doing here. The child must know and that must be why he is crying, I thought.

Before I looked outside, I looked at the people's faces. Some sighed and put their heads in their hands, some looked the other way, but most of them just stared, expressionless. I was confused as to why people were so anxious in this situation. Sure, it didn't look nice, but everyone has seen a muddy field before.

I came to the realization that this wasn't an ordinary coach ride. I had seen the stories on the news. I had heard there was a civil war going on, and when houses were bombed by the opposing team, people that could survive were taken to refugee camps, and were not given rights in these conditions. But not once did I think about this happening to us, because of our luxurious life conditions. But it had happened and now we were here. We . I. At this point I realized what was happening. I closed my eyes again, trying to not think. My family were not here. My eyes watered. I tried to tell myself that they'd just gone to another camp, but I knew it wasn't true. There were even spare spaces on the bus. I tried to not think about it, their bodies lying on the cold, hard ground. There was no more point of living. I wiped my eyes on my sleeve, soaking up the tears as they ran down my face.

I think of where I am going. These camps are riddled with disease. Its wet and muddy and there is no education - young illiterate children in mud, freeze almost to death. As much as I would like to shut out these thoughts, I am unable to. I watch the world crash down beside me, and I break down. I scream and cry like a baby. What has happened could be a dream but it's more like a nightmare. This could be a story but it's more like the truth. All these thoughts are going through my brain but then it stops. I no longer scream, I just wail. I no longer cry, I just weep. As I fall asleep, hoping for a different tomorrow, I dream of wild things - worlds of hopes and dreams. But behind all of it, I feel I have betrayed everyone I knew and love. In surviving, I have abandoned them.

PLUMSTEAD

Light, But Strong

By Prudencia Okechukwu (8 AV)

Go on ballet,
See your struggles as friends,
Go on, it's your moment,
Move and move 'til it ends.

Lessons in life;
Learnt to accept it.
Life is tough,
Sometimes positive!

Ballet isn't girly,
Neither childish.
Once you've nailed it,
You have won.

Light as a free butterfly.
Strong as mountains.
An abstract story teller.

Part of the puzzle
Part of the wide universe
Part of the needed.

See ballet as life.
  Stay light, but strong.
    Stay confident.
      Stay yourself.

(this came about after discussing the power of a place of learning and in particular, a ballet school).

Spiritual Meditation

By Venika Hirani (7 MB)

Sometimes I wonder how long I have known
The temple, the beauty and the glory of it.
The luxurious place, a place that I have always
Dreamed of.
A place of wonder, the reason why my life was
Incomplete.
The last piece of the jigsaw.
It is over.
My life.
The Temple.
The golden pillars shining in the glistening sun,
The smile of the Gods created by His
Devotees. The happiness He feels when he sees the glory and worship from within.
It's here...
Let's g-g-go...

The time has come to embrace the inner peace,
The world everyone believed in,
The God everyone worshipped,
The world, God, embracing peace,
A perfect place is the Temple.

Divine worship to the Gods,
The Gods that smile at us,
I just sometimes wish for a world of peace,
Peace, hatred, love, anger.
Which one is written in my destiny?

PRENDERGAST SCHOOL

Drifting through the ocean

By Felix Dale 10N

Whilst drifting through the ocean,
You can hear a soft tune.
The waves seem to be singing,
And soon comes the moon.

Lonely, sailing through the sea,
You can feel a sense of calm.
Although you are all alone,
The word is in your palm.

Where you are you feel at home,
Your mind is telling you to never go back.
You watch the sun fall behind the hills
And soon the sky begins to fade to black.

Maybe one day you'll push away the thoughts
That keep you planted where you stand,
Or maybe you'll stay there forever
        Never once reaching land.

Prisoner of the Playground

By Julia Wojtasinska 8N

Back and forth. My iron chains singing as they swing. I stand and watch the joyous children with their woolly hats bobbling buoyantly as they run on a carpet of blushing leaves. The sound of their laughter carried on the wind and their footsteps follow it. I glance at the rocking horse with its bright blue saddle and a golden mane.

My closest companion; the sand pit, sits at my shoulder. I can still spot buried treasure disguised beneath its surface. Ruby spades and buckets sparkle and shimmer against the damp sand. The little ones swarmed around the pit like butterflies around a flourishing flower.

The sun starts to slowly set in the distance. It sinks beneath the city to sleep and the last rays brighten the fallen leaves that resemble soldiers after a lost battle. Decayed. The children leave and the light is gone.

Oh how quickly a dream can take of its mask and reveal a nightmare.

The park has been abandoned and the bucket and spade are now seeking companionship. I glance at the rocking horse and the joy has been stolen from its eyes.

My iron chains creak with age as they slowly begin to rust.

Sea

By Saule Gagilaite 7P

Standing
In the middle of the beach
Soft sand beneath my bare feet

Looking
Into the distance
Watching sails of boats bobbing up and down

Walking
Towards the blue waves
Which hit the shore and slither back into the deep again

Feeling
The warm upon my face
The gentle breeze surrounding me

Swimming
In the cold, blue waters
No one existing in the world but me.

The Swing

By Ella Freeman 7P

"My socks are too itchy."
"Please carry my coat."
"I think there is a stone in my shoe."

The moaning was carried by the wind. It was a ballet dancer swaying to a symphony, a jogger running a marathon, a salmon swimming upstream.

A set of muddy footprints were fresh on the gravel path. The clean air was a detox from the streets of the city. Blotches of muddled green crowded the country side like a patchwork quilt. It was paradise.

A splintered plank hung from two soggy ropes: a swing. In the mid-noon light it looked oddly appealing. The young children ran up to it tripping over each other's feet as they went.

After everyone had a go on the swing, a much happier version of the family that had been walking beforehand came out of a tunnel of intertwined branches. They strolled into a large emerald field filled with weeds that seemed to fit perfectly with their surroundings. Mole stumps were scattered around the open expanse of green. Stray twigs and branches littered the ground after being torn away from their mother trees by howling winds in vicious storms. The joyful family laughed —the sound as sweet as a baby's smile. They observed amusing bird calls; hopped over dirty, brown puddles and ran to catch leaves daintily fluttering in the wind.

It was starting to get dark as the family made their way back to the car. Stars started to come into view from out of the windows as they made their way home to the dull the concrete streets of the city. By the time they had gotten to the familiar graffiti roads they knew the children in the back snoozed after a tiring day of fun. Dreams filled with green and fresh air flooded their heads.

THOMAS TALLIS

Year 7

The Park

By Abdullahi Gedow

Children laugh and Play
People having lots of fun
Smelling the green grass

My House

By Elliot Kelly

My home is lovely
Spend time with everybody
Express your feelings

The park

By Jessica Punt

Cooking cookies reak the air
I made new friends there
Mountains, hills tumble
Playing football as my belly rumbles

Home is Home

By Tazkia Khanem

Home, what is it to you?
To me, it's where I never feel
Blue. My mum, my
dad, my sister,
I love them lots.
Loto and Baby
They are my
Pets. I love
my home.

On the streets of London

By Tazkia Khanem

Back in the old days
when your nan was still young,
You could leave your doors open
And still have fun.
Everybody knew everyone,
So somebody tell me,
Why we have gone full circle
And trust no one?
We just open our eyes
And close the blinds
to the madness outside.
But at the back of our minds
Why do we question
Why they had died?
A sister, a husband,
A mother, a wife
Another one taken
Too soon by the knife.
Open our eyes
And we might save a life.
Is a knife worth a life?
And is it worth 20 years of yours?

Home

By Melissa Billa

Home is a place to relax,
It's a place to stay together.
It's where feelings can be shown,
No matter who you are.
Home is where love lies,
Where everyone is themselves,
Where we all come together.
Home means everything to me.
It is where
Respect and kindness are,
Where loved ones stay close.
And that is my home!

Albania

By Max

I walk on the beach,
With my favourite cousins,
In Albania
Your expression is allowed,
Beauty surrounds me,
All my cousins are lovely,
Nothing but love.

The Park

By Joe Llewellyn

The Park is where I make new friends,
The park is where I make memories,
The park is where I have fun,
The park is where I bond with my family
The park is where I get new skills,
The park is where I enjoy my life.

The Valley

By Jack Smith

A place for joy
A place for laughter
A place for hiding
A place for freedom
A place to get away
There's no place like the valley.

The Seaside

By Freddy Gidley

Nice blue skies,
Breeze is nice,
Great food by the seaside,
Bucket of fish,
Is on my dish.
No thank you, I'm ok,
I'll have the pasta.

School

By Samuel Brooks

School is chilled
When I play, I play the field
Some lessons get boring
In them all you can hear is children snoring
Some lessons are great,
That's why no one turns up late
That's my school
If you don't come here, you must be a fool.

The world

By Kieran Lee

We live in a massive world
Filled with people with different lives
We live in a massive world
Where babies are born everyday
We live in a massive world.
You drive down the road
Look at houses with people
Look at cars with more people
Seven billion people cover the world
Sixty million cover our country.

It is a massive world.

My bedroom

By Kieran Lee

My room is a peaceful place to be
Where my window has a view I like to see
Whether that's a night starry sky
or a bright blue sky
It's a place where I can rest my mind and eye,
And gaze into the sky
Gaming is something I like
Where I can be goofy and have fun
Or where I can be dumb.
My desk is full of papers,
A revision book as well
I can revise and try to do well
In tests and not fail.
I can also speak to my friend
We can speak and mess around
And that's my hobbies, I do in my room
It's my own world where I can dream
And speak to people that mean a lot to me.

WANSTEAD

The Yo-Yo

By Jermaine Dallas

Vuyo....When my life goes round like a yo-yo
And my answer comes with a big no no
He's always there
So I can get my mojo

He always makes me laugh
He makes me squeeze my lungs
Like I've just been shot with a gun
But just for fun

There is a place, where I feel appreciated
All my feelings are being abbreviated
Into one person

Vuyo. From 8.8
I assure you he's my best mate
There's no-one else that can relate

To him...
For the person that always advise me not to drink gin,
For the person that does deeds instead of sins
For the person who always tell me good job
Even if I don't win

This may not be the longest poem,
This may not be the most detailed poem
At least you get to know about him

Power of the mind

By Finn Hawksworth

There is a place that I call home
I always see it when my eyes are closed
There's no one there except myself
That is what makes it so powerful

When I'm there I feel so free
I'm letting go of what was before
A clean path is laid out for me
What crosses it remains a mystery

Every day after I have left that place
All the power seems to leave me
I wonder if I'll get it back

Whether or not I feel what I feel when I am there
I know that I can always return

Whatever it is that is troubling me
There is always a way out, always a door that's open
That is when I know that I can let go
And that is the power of the mind

The path to power.

By Sara

It will be the only place on earth were you feel free, safe , loved.
It will be the only place on earth where you discover your true and only power.
Because when you look down into the puppy's eyes you find all the power you need.
Because your power is special , unique. Weather you feel powerful because you're scared and you fight back.
Or... your powerful because your safe and have nothing to worry about , and you use that to your advantage.
And then, you fall, not knowing where to go, and then fight back , control yourself and never forget the puppy whose eyes gave you power to continue the path to the future , the path to power.

Your place

By Finn Hawksworth

Finding a place,
An easy thing to find,
A powerful place to find,
Your heart is free to decide.

Society will push you here and there,
But you must stand and stay where you stick,
What you desire, what you feel,
Whether you are gay or lesbian,
It doesn't matter what anyone says.

Who are you,
Dream your dream,
Be who you are,
Be strong,
Be powerful.

A billion places,
A trillion spaces,
So follow your path,
And let no one get in the way.

One day London will have justice

By Carys Gray

In my bedroom, I think of London,
and the power it holds:
power of women,
and inequality,
Will my mind be misled?
Or will I stand for my beliefs?
Without the women of the past,
would there be a vote for us?
Why is women's football not as important?
Why do men dominate society?
Women are strong,
and have ideas,
so the world should listen up,

in my bed I think of London,
and the power it holds,
thoughts of protest in previous London,
to London changing to hatred,
London's knife crime rising in numbers,
the gangs thinking they have all the power,
but everyone will rise above,
and find a way to stop the crime,
London's strong,
London's fierce,
knife crime will stop,
and no one will have fear,
everybody will come together,
full of power,
to stop the knives striking again.
London is powerful,
from history to now.

Flames of remembrance

By Amelia Hartt

Still smelling the **fire's** scent;
we **remember** everyone that lent
help to the **survivors** that escaped.
Causing us to be the **power** it made.
Remembering what everyone who **died** meant.
Saving people we love from the roar of the **flames**.
Trying hard not to give **anyone** the blame.
We can come **together** as one,
remembering what everyone has done.
Grenfell has no shame!

Nuclear Energy

By Amelia Hartt

Nuclear energy,
what do you think you are doing?
Do you know?
It seems as if you don't.
Chernobyl, what happened there?
You lost control,
it effected hundreds,
made them move out of their homes,
it even killed some.
When it goes wrong,
and the radioactive waves escape,
you can't see them,
but the area becomes uninhabitable.
Radioactive waves from these nuclear plants can kill when let loose,
and you say it is better for the environment,
but it takes millions of years to get rid of the waste,
do you think that that is good for the planet?
But when everyone is gone,
nature takes over, buildings become a place for vines to climb,
weeds appear from the cracks in the paving stones,
and trees begin to grow.
Why can't you find other ways to make energy,
ways that don t hurt people,
ways that don't harm the planet,
ways that don't take such dangerous risks,
ways that are safe for us and the planet.

Breathe

By Livi Kolinsky

Forget about the outside,
Channel out the fear inside,
Smile,
If society doesn't love you, you have to love yourself.
Breathe
Find your place your special place.
Don't give up,
When times get tough,
Forget about the outside
Channel out the fear inside.

Imagine your happy place
Up high in the mountains,
Feeling free among the clouds.
Power ridden,
A sense of pride,
Pride you never had,
Don't think about the pressure,
Forget,
Forget all,
Fight the fear,
Relax,
Breathe.
This is your place your special place.
Forget about the outside,
Channel out the fear inside.

Then you have to go,
Go back to the place that you loathe,
To the people you hate,
The people you hate to know
And they make you remember,
The things you forgot,
And you soon find yourself losing the plot,
The power you gained was hard to bare.
And you begin to spiral into despair.
You wish you were back in the place you once knew.
The one with the mountains and the snow
The one that means everything to you.
But that's gone along with your pride and your power,
You can't forget about the outside,

And you crack under pressure,
Your smile is turned,
Your sadness grew,
And the fear becomes just too overwhelming for you.

Streets of London

By Sofiya Khan-Ringshaw

I look around me, within the swarm of buzzing people,
bright yellow Selfridge's bags catching my attention through the corner of my
eye.
Laughing and smiling, content with their purchases, people walk into the
shops, the warm blast of air against their faces and music in their ears.
Alongside me, giggling children accompanied by their mums sit happily at the
top of the gleaming red double-decker buses, breathing onto the windows
and drawing smiley faces while looking at the beauty of the streets that they
can see.
The sound of chatting amongst the people around me, the beeping of car
horns, the music in my ears filling me with happiness. While the sweet, floral
scent of perfume escaping the doors of shops onto the street.
It seems like the whole world is on that street, filled with happiness, until you
turn the corner onto a small alleyway and the dark reality for many people hits
you.
Away from all the life on the streets of London, are the cold, hungry people,
who don't even have enough money to eat, let alone buy luxuries.
The hours go by, as if the clocks have stopped and they are stuck in this
moment forever. While the cold air whips against their faces, and their
stomachs churn with hunger, they are forced to sit there and watch the world
go by in front of their eyes.
The life's between the people with nothing but a sleeping bag, and those who
are carrying collections of designers bags could not be more different. To most
people, those without roofs over their heads become invisible to them,
as if they are no longer part of their society.

Into the Darkness

By Sofiya Khan-Ringshaw

I climb to the top,
A smile cascades my face.
I'm here,
The place I know I'm meant to be,
Where I am not subject to humiliation,
A place where I can be anything, anyone.

I'm finally there,
But something's not right,
My heart begins to pound uncontrollably,
And then it hits me.
An unwanted feeling swallows me whole,
Leaving the dark presence to infect my soul.

I look to the sky,
The stars do not glimmer,
And things that seem to be beautiful once,
Only seem to bring unhappiness now.
I can feel the struggle pushing me down,
It begins to cecum me.
An indescribable feeling of regret and downfall,
Leaving me alone and weak.

Now I see something.
A small light,
A glimmer of hope.
I begin to run faster and faster.
I try to reach it and I know that I'm really close,
And then it's gone.
It disappears into the dismal surrounding.
Now I know I know the inevitability of the darkness.

This Needs to Stop

By Shakira Warburton Ofori-Duah.

Okay, this needs to stop.
First it was slavery,
Then segregation,
Now a load of racism.
This isn't right,
Just because I'm not you,
Doesn't mean I'm different.
We could be the same,
Just open your eyes.

Beautiful, powerful, water

By Zaini M

It wonders through the trees,
Hikes through the mountains,
It's on a journey- a mission,
It is beautiful,
It is powerful,
The River

It tumbles from great heights,
Never afraid to fall,
Cool and crisp
Light but strong,
It is beautiful,
It is powerful,

The Water-fall

By Zaini M

It covers the globe, like a robe
It is home to so many creatures
It's as old as time herself,
It is beautiful,
It is powerful,
The ocean

It courses through my veins,
Makes my identity,
It's in me,
It is me,
Beautiful, powerful, Water.

Minds and Places

By Zaini M

Looking far beyond,
Wondering what will happen.
Minds whizzing, brains buzzing,
Darkness swallowing you whole.
Not knowing what will happen.
Not knowing what has happened.
Not knowing what is coming.

Finding yourself and who you are.
Where you belong.
Your place.
Your role.
Your part.

Anyone can do anything.
Everyone has the ability to do everything.
You can conquer all, become anything
Be who you want to be.

Finding yourself can be scary.
Your place and where you belong.
Your mind works in a million different ways.
Everyone is different.

Everyone is unique.
Everyone is powerful.
Everyone has a place,
But finding that place is a different question.

Something that only the mind can do.

I'm upset.
People need homes
People need help
Not a bunch of adults 'trying to get down our through our throughts'
You don't know a thing about us

You hate on other political parties
There are people sitting on the streets with no family
I'm angry
I'm vexed
And really upset I can't stand this disrespect
You say you will make change
Do it
We are human
Right?
We need a person in charge
 of keeping us safe, happy and free
not throwing shade like your 15

you're a grown up
sooo grown up
stop beings selfish
and start treating the people who aren't rich or wealthy
like how you treat the one that are full of money
we are all equal, we are all the same but just have different ambitions
but how can someone be so evil that they can't make a single good decision
so don't let the fame and fortune get to your brain
I'm angry
I'm vexed
And really upset I can't stand this disrespect
You say you will make change
Do it
We are human
Right?

Don't Bully!

By Kylah Sergeant

Bullying is not fair,
Everyone should be treated with care,
Just think! About the people you hurt,
Before you treat someone like dirt,
Why would you even dare?

Be
United
Love and
Lean on
Yourself

How do you know what is going on in peoples head,
Many people feel alone but just because you don't see or think it doesn't mean
there okay.

The thing people don't understand is that everyone has feelings,
Just because they're not you, doesn't mean that there weird or disgusting.

Don't be jealous of raw talent or of something that you don't like,
Because being harmful to someone won't help you achieve power

One Girl and Her Poem

By Kennedy Gibbons

I've been given this place,
On this page of this book,
One poem written by one girl,
In this one place,
I can write anything,
I can write about the days when I wake up,
Wishing I didn't,
Or the days where I can't stop smiling,
Or I can write about how I feel like there's so much expected of me,
That my academic progress comes before me.
I can write about how I have no place,
No place to preach, cry or sin.
But now I do.
I can write about whatever and whomever I desire,
I can humiliate the ones who've humiliated me,
Hurt the ones who have hurt me.
But this is a place of power;
Power shouldn't be used for your own needs,
Power should be used for the greater good.
So I forgive those whose pushed me down,
Because now I'm standing.
Now I have the power you once had,
Now I give the power back to you,
And I give it to everyone who breathes on this planet.
Because if everyone has power,
Then there is no power,
Then everyone is equal,
That's why this is a place of power;
I'm just one girl and her poem.

Made in the USA
Columbia, SC
03 September 2018